Viviana

Viviana lives through the persecution of Christians
until Emperor Constantine's endorsement
of the first Nicene Creed in 325

Nathan Driscoll

malcolm down

PUBLISHING

First published 2025 by Malcolm Down Publishing Ltd.
www.malcolmdown.co.uk

28 27 26 25   7 6 5 4 3 2 1

British Library Cataloguing in Publication Data
A catalogue record for this book is available from the British Library.

ISBN 978-1-917455-23-7

Cover design by Esther Kotecha
Art direction by Sarah Grace

Printed in the UK

Dedication

For my wife, Jenny, and my friend Tim.
I could not have brought this story to fruition
without their encouragement and advice.

Contents

Acknowledgements

When I write a story, I start with an idea, a character and usually a beginning scene, but not an overall plan. I talk to my wife as I go along and the story begins to unfold in my mind. Her perceptive comments prompt me to think of developmental ideas and when the script is first drafted, she reads through it thoughtfully, pointing out the parts which are not clear. Without her invaluable support I would be travelling completely in the dark.

My friend Tim has, as ever, greatly helped me with my scripts both technically and substantively but has gone much further. He recognises that my attempts to write stories are not part of an ambition to become a novelist but rather to use dramatic narrative as a means of exploring the human condition at certain points in our histories. More than that, they are a means of self-exploration as I wrestle with what works and what doesn't work in my own faith, my own story and the hopes and fears of those I know of.

I could not translate that self-exploration into print without the support of Malcolm Down and his publishing team. Malcolm and his publishing colleague, Sarah Grace, enable unknown writers like me to have a voice. Every script is assessed on its own merits and this is done for me by Sheila Jacobs who goes on to edit the final script. The assessment process is not always easy but it always results in an improved flow and inter-connectedness within the narrative. Thanks to Sheila for her meticulous attention to detail which readers always benefit from. Many thanks also to Sarah Grace and Esther Kotecha for their imaginative artwork.

Finally, thanks to my many friends who take an interest and read my books. I am very grateful.

Preface

As I wrote this, I became more troubled, along with everyone around me, about the conflicts in Ukraine and the Middle East. I began to feel increasingly affected by the 'game of chess' being played with people's lives and I found myself writing an imaginary letter to a world leader as if I were a victim on the ground in one of the many war zones we hear about on the news:

Dear...

Is a piece of land worth my son's life? When innocent people are caught up in a conflict, they are murdered. Why don't we call it murder anymore?

My voice, like millions of others, is drowned out by sirens and explosions, but history will not judge you by your own standards – you *will* be judged by those who look back on how much good you did and to what extent you valued each life; not how many you killed, how much land you conquered and how rich your country was.

We have now forgotten what peace ever looked like. For now all we have is grief, injury, the houses we used to live in and memories of a better life; you have the luxury of protection and the adrenalin of power – the only people who will remember you with affection are people like you; yes, people who justify killing. Yes, I feel bitter but I will not let that bitterness destroy my soul – as it has yours...

Even as I spilled out my frustration, I knew there was a connection between the story I have written, set in the fourth century, and our world's current troubles. The connection is simply this: is human nature the same as it ever was? Are the opposing instincts of power seeking and reconciliation still wrestling with one another?

The story runs over twenty-five years starting with life under the Roman emperor Diocletian in 302. The characters in the family are imagined but the history is true – references to the Roman emperors, bishops and the creed itself are taken from academic sources.[1]

As the story is read, comparisons can be made with today's conflict-ridden world – technology, scientific advance, the nation state and modern democracy have developed beyond all measure in many parts of the world since the year 300 but is the spectrum of kindness, indifference and cruelty just the same as it ever was? How does the Church position itself? Is it a voice of conscience or compliance? Do both the Church and State fully recognise their own self-interest in the ways they manage their subjects?

The story follows the lives of a sister and a brother by 'visiting' their lives at various stages, when they are teenagers, then young adults and finally years later.

- Part One takes place *inside the family* during the persecution of Christians.

- Part Two takes place after the persecution stops *inside the church community*. It describes in part how the Church sought to provide an alternative way of living compared to the wider culture of the time.

---

1. I will provide a short historical note before the story begins and list my chief sources at the end. The records of Christ's life and the letters to the early churches only became the *New Testament* in the very late fourth century, more than 350 years after Christ. Prior to that they were used as working documents and spiritual guides but were only fully joined to the Old Testament as the complete divinely inspired Scriptures in 393 and 397 at the Councils of Hippo Regius and Carthage respectively. See Frederick Fyvie Bruce, *The New Testament Documents: Are They Reliable?* (San Francisco, CA: Bottom of the Hill Publishing, 2013), p. 25.

- Part Three is when the *Church and State combine* in 325 when the Nicene Creed is both authorised by the Church and endorsed by the emperor Constantine.

Finally, the intensity of feeling which divided the Church in the fourth century was very deep; the balance between what to believe and how to behave has always exercised the Church in every age. The other never-ending preoccupation for the Church has been how closely it should align itself with the State. In peacetime the relationship can be uncomfortable – in war time it becomes crucial.

Introduction:
Historical Note

The early Christian Church was encouraged to submit to the authorities. St Paul wrote this to the Roman Church:

> Let everyone be subject to the governing authorities, for there is no authority except that which God has established. The authorities that exist have been established by God. Consequently, whoever rebels against the authority is rebelling against what God has instituted, and those who do so will bring judgment on themselves.

This submission included being persecuted for one's faith and counting it as joy. As St Paul said to the Thessalonian church:

> Therefore, among God's churches we boast about your perseverance and faith in all the persecutions and trials you are enduring.[2]

Put simply, early Christians were expected to be ready to die without protest for their faith. Later on, Christians challenged the wrongdoing of their governments as they realised they could not fight for justice without doing so. William Wilberforce's fight against the institution of slavery was a case in point. Christ had provided an example by challenging the hypocrisy of the Jewish leadership in his own day. Christians also, regrettably, became aligned with political factions and rulers to the point where they were simply adjuncts to the political

---

2. 2 Thessalonians 1:4.

ambitions of their masters. There were twenty-five popes up to the year 1059. Of these, twenty-one were appointed by emperors.[3]

In the first few centuries after Christ, Christians found themselves in the middle of a culture of pagan worship; that culture was infused with a great deal of Greek influence, in which knowledge of all kinds was held in far greater esteem than the physical and material world. Various gods had special interests such as fertility, hunting, agriculture, motherhood, death and rebirth. Some Christians believed that God was inaccessible and had sent a holy representative, Christ, to the world; these Christians, called Arians, were in conflict with those who believed that Christ was eternal.

The emperors, however, were more interested in the gods who would bring them victory in battle. Jupiter, Sol Invictus and Mars were such gods. The Roman Empire at the beginning of the fourth century was under the control of two emperors with several Caesars under them. Military might and the ability to keep the army on your side by paying them well were of prime importance.

Constantine became the sole emperor of the Roman Empire in 324 when he defeated Licinius with whom he had been previously sharing the empire. His attraction to the God of the Christians was based on the fear that to annoy that God could affect his military success. He cared little about doctrinal divisions, preferring the flexibility to switch to whichever side would better suit his strategy at the time.

There is a widely held story that Constantine saw a vision of Christ in 312 when he won a crucial battle against Maxentius just outside Rome at Milvian Bridge. This story was written by Bishop Eusebius of Caesarea in his biography of Constantine after 325.

---

3. Please see Francis Fukuyama, *The Origins of Political Order* (London: Profile Publishing, 2011). Please also see my book, Nathan Driscoll, *Reformation* (Welwyn Garden City: Malcolm Down Publishing, 2024) for an insight into the entwining of the Church and State in the sixteenth century.

Biographies or Panegyrics were rewritten histories which gave flawless descriptions of their subjects. Constantine was happy to be compared with Alexander the Great, Moses, the apostles and even Christ himself. To criticise an emperor would be tantamount to committing suicide. So even if Constantine did see the vision, there is no way of verifying it as genuine. It is far more likely that it was manufactured, fully or partially, as part of Eusebius' panegyric. Evidence from coinage and archaeological finds indicate that Constantine was still prepared to be blessed by Sol Invictus long after the battle of Milvian Bridge. Constantine's slaughter of the Franks in 312, the murders of Licinius and his family in 324, and Constantine's wife, Fausta, and son, Crispus in 326 are well attested.

As already mentioned in the preface, the New Testament Canon was not sealed, despite copies of the Gospels and apostolic letters being circulated between the churches. To be a Christian required adherence to a set of beliefs about God and Christ. With no fully agreed New Testament to refer to, there were many different variations both in belief and practice. This was a challenge that Constantine never managed to conquer – he constantly pleaded with the bishops throughout the empire to put their doctrinal differences about Christ aside in order to appease God.

In the story, slavery is discussed at a church meeting. It is worth noting that Gregory of Nyssa (c 335-c 395) was strident in his opposition to slavery as an institution; unlike his predecessors, from inside and outside Christianity, and as far as recorded history is concerned, Gregory's was a lone voice.[4]

The two key questions which exercised the Church were, firstly, whether Christ was eternally part of the Godhead or simply a perfect

---

4.   See Tom Holland, *Dominion* (London: Little Brown, 2019), p. 124.

created being, and secondly, what to do with those who had lapsed during the persecutions but wanted to come back into the Church.

From 325 when the Nicene Creed was first created, Athanasius, who became the leading proponent of Christ being of the same substance or essence as the Father, was exiled five times when emperors acceded to pressure from bishops to change the official teaching of the Church. Athanasius died in 373. Apart from a brief period of persecution under Julian the Apostate from 361-363, the rulers allowed Christianity to continue.

As far as the Creed is concerned, it would take until the Council of Constantinople in 381, forty-three years after Constantine's death, for the theological disputes over Christ's status to finally rest; the interim years would be full of shifting sands, exiles and pronouncements, depending on who could most effectively curry favour with the Roman emperor. The Niceno-Constantinopolitan Creed of 381 finally described Christ as being 'of one essence with the Father'.

The Eastern Roman Empire in the Early 4th Century where the story takes place

PART 1

Persecution

Chapter One

Life or Death? The Year 302 in Nicomedia, Asia Minor

Fourteen-year-old Viviana and her brother, Columba, looked down from the top storey of their building as their mother, Phyllis, was dragged away by the Roman soldiers. The sound of her screams would never fully leave Viviana, especially in the darkness of night.

Viviana, two years older than Columba, tried to comfort him but it was to no avail. For the last five years, since being told of his father's death on the battlefield, it was as if his childhood had been stolen; he had built up an imaginary vision of his father which had then been shattered into a million pieces. Viviana felt him push her away with his pent-up anger.

They ran to their aunt, Clara, telling her what had happened. Because they were associated with the Christians, all they could do was hide. Viviana shook with fear – what would happen to her mother? How could she live without her? She prayed all night for God to protect her and bring her back home to them; quietly sobbing, she clung onto Clara. Later as she lay awake, she thought she could smell the dungeon her mother was in.

Phyllis was thrown onto the ground; the side of her face was torn to shreds by the rough sand. It was dark, frightening and the smell of human waste was everywhere. She thought she had been blinded until her eyes adjusted. The other prisoners took no notice of her arrival, not even looking up; they were as good as dead and wished they were. Together the thieves, adulterers, deserters, runaway slaves and the few Christians were simply one tormented mass of flesh. It was freezing cold in this pit of human degradation and the cacophony of low groaning sounded like an unending eternal hell.

Phyllis could hear wild dogs yelping as they were being fed with raw meat. In a short time, *she* would be the raw meat, torn to pieces for the delight of the crowd and more importantly because of the emperor's *divine* will. Perhaps it could all be sidestepped if she were to sign the certificate agreeing to worship the Roman gods rather than her own cherished Christian God. Diocletian, the emperor, could only be shown loyalty through complete subjection – anything else was betrayal. If the people were to worship him, as they were required to, they had also to worship the gods of his choosing.

Five years before, Phyllis would have gladly signed her soul away but what had happened since then was to change her life irrevocably. She had never even thought about why Christians seemed to welcome suffering; they had a hope which seemed to transcend human misery. Kissing the wall was something she had heard Christians did as a witness to other prisoners, so she kissed it hoping that she might be miraculously lifted out of the dungeon. It was not to be. Remembering back to the first time she had been to a gathering of Christians, she recalled that she didn't really know what they believed but there was a sense of purpose – then she began to hear what Christ had taught, the story of his crucifixion and resurrection. It took hold of her and she prayed for her own heart and mind to be transformed. Her emotions and moods were like a leaden rock but now the Holy Spirit touched her soul. She felt a volcanic inner change. There was now a purpose in her life which she had never experienced before; she was consumed. In some small way she felt wary about surrendering her soul, but it was better than trudging towards death in the cold, unrelenting storm clouds of poverty looking after the children and baking bread for a few sesterius.[5]

In the darkness she found two or three others who she thought were Christians. One spat at her before she realised her mistake. The other two made the sign of the cross and one of them, who she discovered was named Phoebe, weakly held out her hand. Her daughter was called Eunice. With her head bowed, Eunice began to pray and Phyllis was struck by her fervour. It sounded as if she was an Old Testament prophet: 'Our Father God, who came to meet us on this dry and dusty earth in the form of your Son, we praise you that you have prepared for us a heavenly city where cruelty and violence cannot breathe; for now, those wild dogs will have their moment of false glory.'

She paused as if she were waiting for the Holy Spirit to help her. Then she copied Christ's prayer: 'Father, forgive them, for they know not what they do'[6] – when he was on the cross. 'Lord, even now open the eyes of these blind men who think they are invincible...'

In an instant, Eunice was breathless on the ground; the force of the blow was such that she could not speak even though she tried to. Phyllis went to her aid and the man who had struck Eunice spat at them.

'We do not want to hear about your stupid dreams!' he shouted. 'Why are you tormenting us when we are already broken and waiting to die? Wait for the dogs to tear you up and pray your delusions to the emperor – we will all die, in here or in the arena, the sooner the better. Stop your ranting, or I will kill you myself!'

---

5. A very small denomination of Roman currency.
6. Luke 23:34, ESV.

Phyllis saw the rage in the man's eyes and it sparked something inside her. In the midst of the filth around them she had nothing to lose. She looked straight at him: 'You are frightened to die, aren't you? This woman is not. You can punch her, you can kill her – but you cannot kill her spirit. You are already dead; why don't you turn your heart towards God and let his Spirit change you?'

The man sneered and then carried on to where he had been lying down. None of the other prisoners stirred. Phyllis helped Eunice sit up and after a while asked her how she and her mother had ended up there. She told Phyllis that two soldiers had come for them after another believer had given their whereabouts away. She held out her hand to Phyllis and found the strength to carry on talking: 'Our only solace is that we are together. I cannot be separated from my mother – we have lived together and now we must die together. When our father died, we lost our livelihood; the local believers took us in and saved our lives.' And then Eunice asked Phyllis, 'What about you?'

Phyllis felt a strange sense of uncertainty as she told Eunice that her husband, Bonitus, had decided the only way to escape from their downtrodden life was to become a soldier. Barbarians from the north had invaded Roman lands and he went off. He had come back injured but insisted on going back and died later, so she was told. Now her voice became stronger: 'I was angry with the emperor when he claimed the victory by the power of Jupiter – the god who let my husband die; was I supposed to worship Jupiter for that? My daughter was just three and my son was born a few months after my husband left to go back to the army. So if I die for my faith, I will also die for my husband's memory. I did not keep my thoughts to myself. The soldiers heard about my anger and came for me – but I have had to leave my children behind. By God's grace they are at my sister's house. She is a single woman and she is also a believer.'

The rats began to explore the excrement in the corner – it was to their taste and several more came to join the feast. They had the freedom to come and go as they pleased, but if Phyllis were to sign over her loyalty to the emperor she would 'become' one of those rats; free, but only free to worship the gods who had allowed her husband to die in battle. Was it her anger or her faith that drove her? She was not certain and was sucked deeper into the confusion of self-doubt. The difference between night and day was marginal as the light could only enter the cavern through the iron grating at the top of the underground dungeon. As the hours went by, Phyllis became more and more disorientated as a result of being without water or food. She lay down and in a half-sleep started to wander into the past. The side of her face felt as if it had already been ravaged by a wild dog; some of the grit had embedded itself in her skin. Through the moans of the other prisoners, she could hear her husband's voice even though she knew he was dead: 'What is our life? Misery? I could join Diocletian's army and make a name for myself. The mighty leaders of Rome have risen from nowhere; think of Diocletian himself, Constantine in the west and his father, Constantius – were they not ordinary men who turned themselves into gods? How did they? I can do the same. I know I can.'

Phyllis remembered the day when he kissed her and marched off – thinking to herself, 'Will I see him again? Is this madness?' Intermittent memories filtered through:

I look up and see him hobbling towards our mud-built shack. There is no regiment behind him; he stumbles and falls. I run and help him up. 'I will go back,' I hear him say.

I am looking for him again – but he isn't there . . .

Still semi-conscious, Phyllis passed out and then revived a little:

Singing mixed with the sound of battle. Who is telling me this, or am I imagining it? Bonitus is on the ground and a horse from his own side tramples on him – the shriek of pain – one of his own soldiers stops and decides to put him out of his misery with one thrust of the sword. Is this true? He is dead, I am sure...

Eating the bread and fruit one of the Christian folk bring when we are so hungry – the hope of heaven away from the torment of living – the battle cries have faded and the worship and singing increase...

The door opened and some bread, cheese and a few chunks of pork were given to Phyllis, Phoebe and Eunice; before they could touch it, two of the rats were there: Phyllis fisted them away and began to eat; much of it came back up. Phoebe was too weak to eat and Eunice was able to take some. The guard beat away the other prisoners so none of the others could steal it from them, for the Christians had to be strong enough to fight the dogs if it were to be the kind of spectacle the emperor desired. He wanted his noblemen and their wives to be impressed; exhausted broken bodies would simply be like dogs eating raw meat.

After the food, Phyllis lay down and for a moment fell asleep, but was awakened by the sound of a young girl and a boy from outside. 'Please, no...' was all she heard.

'Are they my children?' she thought and then shouted out: 'Viviana ... Columba?'

The thought that the emperor's men did what they wanted to with the children of the Christians, and not just the Christians, kept coming back.

'What am I doing? Am I out of my mind?'

The reality of what she was about to do struck at something deep inside her and she lay down again. She could not sleep; what if they had taken her children to appease their lust? She asked herself if she should stay alive and be there for her children at the cost of betraying her fellow believers, and forcing herself to worship Jupiter, at least in public. Loyalty to her children meant betrayal to the fellowship – what did she owe to Phoebe and Eunice who were so pure in heart?

My children might not be looked after by Clara – what if the soldiers do the same to her and bring her here? They might be fed to the wild beasts because they were known to be the children of a Christian – they might simply die for want of food and water – it would have been easier if I had been barren. But now I have to choose . . .

What will I be asked to do to prove that I am genuine? They will make me worship Jupiter in front of their eyes. Even if I am sincere, will that count for anything?

What does God want me to do? Some would say I should do anything to protect my children – after all, they were given to me by God. The moment has come. If I refuse to deny Christ, I will make my children orphans. I cannot do that – I cannot do that – I cannot do that . . .

She shouted, 'Guard, guard – I have to tell you something, now!'

No one came for hours but when the door opened, she told the guard that she would sign the certificate to honour the emperor and his gods. Phyllis could not meet Phoebe and Eunice's glances as she was taken out of the cavern and kept in another cellar; she could hear the dogs and now the roar of two lions. She loved her children but her 'betrayal' of Phoebe and Eunice overtook her thoughts. And what about her Lord, himself? Yes, his mother and brothers were around him when he was crucified, but he did not have any children – could she take any comfort in that? Phyllis sensed that the day of the emperor's celebration was near; her fate was in his hands.

Will I be spared? Will I see my children again?

Chapter Two
The Amphitheatre

Diocletian had won the title of Roman emperor in the year of 284; he was ruthless. He had his own Praetorian[7] prefect killed, and the person who had helped him carry out the murder was then murdered at Diocletian's behest. It was a world where loyalty could only be a transient tool in acquiring and holding onto power. Roman emperors did not value generosity of spirit; at best it was a form of camouflage in the way a praying mantis hides itself by changing colours to fit in with the surrounding leaves before pouncing on its prey. But emperors had to be watchful that they themselves did not become victims to other predators; army generals and family members were like the bats and dogs that feed on the praying mantis. No one had closer access to an emperor than his wife; the female praying mantis eats the male shortly after mating. Every thwarted act of treachery raised the level of fear; anyone's life had to be dispensable for an emperor to survive.

It was not simply the stories of catastrophe and fear that pervaded every level of the empire – the conquests of foreign tribes and lands were also reflected in the symbolic entertainment in the amphitheatre. The passions of the common people were held captive and then diverted into regular psychodramas sealed by the blood of the victims and the agonising spectacle of death; watching and absorbing the pain and suffering of others had become a habit. Animal sacrifice, gladiatorial combat, public execution and the gory tearing up of Christians conveyed images of how the divinely appointed emperor saw life and death. More acutely, no one was left in any doubt as to

---

7. The Praetorian Guards were the bodyguards and the officers providing intelligence for the emperor.

what the rules of conformity were. The amphitheatre was carved out of a hillside. There were three tiers, the one nearest to ground level for the nobility, the middle tier for men of some standing and the highest tier for women and children. The lowest level contained a raised dais where the emperor and his consort would sit. Those close to the emperor would be seated nearby, protected by a barrier from the dust bowl but close enough to hear every scream and see every drop of blood; for the nobility the art of sycophancy was essential.

Two gladiators came into the arena – they had been selected from a pool of slaves. Muscled and bare-chested, they strode into the centre of the amphitheatre. Their vaunting expressions initially showed no hint of fear. Gladiatorial fights were brutal; they were a prequel to the blood lust of the crowd which would be fully satisfied by the later animal baiting and the goring of Christians. Nevertheless, each gladiator knew that they could be wounded, in both their pride and their flesh, so they were desperate to win, as their lives actually did depend on it; sometimes they would perish. The first gladiator to be forced to the ground would draw shouts of derision from the crowd.

Diocletian remained expressionless except for the occasional smile, thinking back to his own younger self. As his physical prowess lessened, the extent to which he could enjoy exacting revenge increased; his capacity for cruelty had grown exponentially over the last two decades. The nobles and generals who instantly smiled when he did were the ones he held under the greatest suspicion.

The two men were now both on the ground, struggling for dominance over each other. Suddenly one of them let go of his dagger and the other thrust his into the stomach of his opponent. The wounded man pulled out the dagger and tried to thrust it back but the victor had rolled away and stood up triumphant. He raised his arms and kicked his opponent back onto the ground. The contest was over and the defeated gladiator was pulled away by his feet. The crowd laughed as he was dragged away. The victor would be kept healthy until the next games, but how many victories would he need to be set free?

The next event began with a gladiator baiting a lion. The man tried to spear the hungry beast with a spear but missed. The lion jumped and almost tore the man's neck from his head; the lion was soon outnumbered by three more gladiators. One of the spears brought a spurt of blood from the lion's shoulder and after a few minutes, the noble animal weakened and further blows were delivered. The crowd cheered as the lion slumped to the ground and its eyes slowly closed. The gladiator and the lion were dragged out of the arena unceremoniously.

Now the wild dogs came into the arena, and Phoebe and Eunice were pushed in from a gate at the side. Eunice tried to protect her mother but it was to no avail. The dogs smelt the blood as both Phoebe and Eunice had been slashed on their backs beforehand – the rags they were wearing barely covered them. Diocletian stood up to applaud as the dogs clustered round them, now both barely alive.

'Where is your Saviour now?' he bellowed out.

As soon as he stood and applauded, the crowd followed suit, with shouts of acclamation and praise for the emperor. The wild dogs were herded into their cages as they were tempted back by some bait; they could not resist the soft internal organs of deer and antelopes. Phyllis was now led into the arena – near to her were Phoebe and Eunice's torn bodies; Phoebe was still alive.

An Oath Stone was placed in front of Phyllis – she was not chained but ordered to swear allegiance to *Iuppiter* in front of the stone. She duly complied and was about to turn away when a guard stood and blocked her path. Another guard dragged Phoebe to just below the emperor's balcony and gave Phyllis a spear.

'Now offer this Christian as a sacrifice to *Iuppiter* and say these words; repeat after me,' he said.

He began and Phyllis repeated the lines in a soft trembling voice. 'Louder!' he bellowed. 'No one can hear you.'

He began again. 'I offer this sacrifice to *Iuppiter, his fellow gods* and to you, O masterful emperor, in total submission and obedience. I reject the heinous lies of the Christians forever.'

Phyllis repeated the words as loud as she could and looked over at Phoebe on the ground, groaning and twitching.

'Do it!' gasped Phoebe. 'I want to go home; I bear you no malice – go, care for your children.'

Phyllis hesitated and brought the spear down but it was not forceful enough to kill the twitching Phoebe. The guard now snatched the spear from Phyllis and killed Phoebe with a single swift stab through the heart.

Phyllis was handcuffed and gagged and taken to the side of the arena by two burly guards. Emperor Diocletian stood up. Immediately there was absolute silence.

'This woman has recanted her faith and on the face of it, complied with the oath of allegiance. What say you whether she should be spared or not? I wish to hear from you, Gallus, and you, Callipas.'

The emperor sat down. Gallus was first to rise; he was a young nobleman anxious to ingratiate himself with the emperor.

'My master and lord, only you have the divine wisdom to decide. My view is that to spare her will allow other Christians the opportunity to practise their treacherous faith and then recant at the last minute. We cannot allow this treasonous sect to subvert the authority of the emperor.'

With that he bowed towards Diocletian and sat down. Now Callipas, one of Diocletian's advisors, stood up to respond. He had had the benefit of hearing Gallus' submission. He did not want to be overshadowed by him and so deliberately took a different approach, even though he actually agreed with him.

'If the pledge of allegiance to the emperor and the gods is to mean anything, then those who sign it should be given the chance to prove their sincerity. For if not, then we will have no way to test if anyone is true in their subjugation to our lord and master, the emperor. How, otherwise, will we be able to root out the die-hards in the Christian sect? If they return to their religion they should be brought back here for their punishment and it should be three times as painful as this.'

Callipas and Gallus and many others had anticipated that the emperor would use the occasion to test out their loyalty. Any such public questioning meant the stakes were very high. The emperor was suspicious of them both; Gallus because of his sycophancy laced with a hint of murderous ambition, and Callipas, who had recently been spending a lot of time with some of the senior military commanders. Diocletian stood up again. The silence came instantly but with an intense menace in the air.

'This woman is in fear and trembling for her life. She could not even speak out the pledge clearly without being goaded; she did not have the strength to carry out the sacrifice. Of course, Gallus, she could be spared if she were unknowing about anything, but you have not the courage to make an individual judgement about her demeanour. Is your judgement based on rhetoric alone? Are you so in fear of me that you are unable to say what you think about her? What is your reckoning of human nature? Are you too weak to voice an opinion?'

Gallus looked down as the emperor spoke and left the amphitheatre very quickly. Diocletian continued, 'Callipas, the pledge to me and the gods is not designed to test out Christians who are wavering but to establish the core instincts of those peoples we have been given divine authority to conquer, that is, those who have not previously been under my rule. The pledge is not a failsafe; it is a confirmation of my natural authority and divinity. Gallus was too weak to make a judgement and you are too cunning for your own good; you do not mean what you say but only wish to distance yourself from Gallus to gain my favour. Your words are worthless.'

Phyllis was left in the arena as two lions were let out; some soft organ tissue from an antelope had been thrown at her. It was enough for the lions to do their worst. The emperor lost interest halfway through Phyllis' terror and retired to drink wine and choose two concubines for the afternoon. The nobles and generals waited until he had left, unconcerned about Phyllis' fate, but mightily relieved that they had not been asked to speak about her by the emperor. That same evening Callipas and his family left and travelled west towards Gaul after dark.

The next day Gallus' 'suicide' was announced. The nobility would all talk publicly about the shame of his reprimand being enough to make him take his own life. Privately they would know that Gallus had been visited by Diocletian's henchmen, the Praetorian Guard, and offered the choice between taking poison or being disembowelled before being quartered, after which his severed head would be put on display. He would take the poison and the 'suicide' would be announced.

The Praetorian Guard also visited Callipas the next day with an ample supply of poison to find that he and his family had left the previous evening. They returned to the palace to consult the emperor. When the emperor woke up from his stupor he was not feeling well; he was told of Callipas' departure and after a few moments just shrugged his shoulders, calling again for one of the concubines from the previous day to come back.

Chapter Three
The Aftermath

Clara stood motionless on the highest tier of the amphitheatre staring blankly at the bloodstained, sandy ground where her sister, Phyllis, had been so brutally savaged. What Clara did not know was that Columba had also crept into the crowd, to watch the soldier pierce his mother taking her last breath; Columba surreptitiously left.

The dispersing crowd had spent several hours inhaling the violence – the toxic blend of fear and laughter would embed itself deep into the folklore of their children's games.

Who would be the victorious gladiator? Who would be the noble lion speared slowly to death? Who would be the helpless Christian torn apart by wild dogs? Most importantly of all, who would be the emperor?

Phyllis' body had been hauled onto a cart with the other corpses and together they were all thrown into a hollow just outside the town. The people could see the pit as they went about their daily business to and from the market. When the stench started to waft more strongly towards the emperor's palace, the hole was filled in.

A few days later, some of the soldiers built a bonfire and an impromptu celebration was held over the filled-in hollow. Some of the common people danced on top of the mass grave as they drank vinegar-infused wine; it could do them no harm to be seen cavorting around in the emperor's honour. If they were noticed by the soldiers and officials, when the next hiatus came, they might be spared. Life was a tapestry of good fortune and disaster, all with a backdrop of unending drudgery; it was as unpredictable as a weathervane changing direction in the wind. Clara and Phyllis, like many others, had lost their parents, who were in their mid-thirties, to the plague.

A few weeks later, Clara went back to the spot and knelt there in silence for as long as she dared; it was late and dark. Looking from side to side every few seconds to begin with, she tried to pray silently. Searching for the right words was fruitless and she felt completely alone. How was she to comfort Phyllis' children?

She remembered how emboldened she had felt when the church was singing and praising together, believing that Christ would return in a matter of weeks; that courage had vanished now. She felt scared and ashamed to admit that she was terrified. She had nothing to offer God except her grief and her fear – and after a few more minutes she got up in despair and began to walk away. As she looked at her feet, she wondered what it must have been like for Phyllis to walk into the amphitheatre, looking down, taking those last few steps.

After a short distance something told her to stop and return to the spot; she wanted the psalm about God being 'close to the broken-hearted' and saving the 'crushed in spirit' to be true for her.[8] She knelt down again, desperately hoping that God would connect with her inner self.

If Christ can forgive the soldiers for setting the dogs onto my sister – can he? – can he not also take away the suffering the children will now have?

Clara could not hear anything in her heart and after a while got up again to return home. That was all she could do, and every so often she would come back to the spot late at night and wait before God for a while. There was no blinding flash but something told her she had to keep coming back there to honour Phyllis if nothing else. Her mind kept wandering back to the children:

What was hidden in their inner selves? Where would their love for their mother go now? Would it turn itself into revenge or imitation –

8. Psalm 34:18.

bitterness or gentleness – warmongering or peacemaking? Which God would win their hearts – Christ or Jupiter? Would Phyllis' death have been for nothing?

The believers no longer met in each other's houses for fear of arrest. The new church building had been razed to the ground by Diocletian, and most of the records of the life of Christ, including the Gospel of Mark and the Gospel of Thomas and letters of St Paul had been confiscated and burnt. For a while the believers had met in each other's houses but now only twos and threes could meet secretly at night, and even then the risks of being seen were very high. Of the fifty or so believers, only a few could read, and there was only one copy of a Gospel account and a few of St Paul's letters hidden away in a cellar belonging to one of the church members. When those small groups of believers met at night, they would spend time memorising as much of the Gospel as they could; they would not sing but prayed silently for many hours. Just before the light peered over the horizon, they would sneak back to their homes and arrive before their children woke up. The older children would often comfort the younger ones if they woke in the night when both the parents were out. They would tell their smaller siblings that they were working at the palace or digging a well for the soldiers.

Viviana was small, quiet and self-contained for her fourteen years. She had a dark complexion with deep blue eyes often hidden by a mop of curly hair. She liked her hair acting as a barrier between her and the rest of the world; all through her childhood she would watch the other children play but rarely join in. When they had called her, she would usually refuse and go off to find her mother. Occasionally she would go when her brother, Columba, persuaded her, but not for long as he would always turn the game into a battle. Since finding out about her mother's gory end, she had hardly spoken. Every night before she closed her eyes she would hold onto a little wooden cross her mother had given to her; in the morning it would still be in her hand. During the day she simply got on with helping with washing and drying the laundry, which Clara did for two of the wealthy households situated higher up at the edge of the city looking down towards the harbour.

The wealthy houses were about a mile away up the hill, built with strong stone and marble, not the mud brick and mortar of their own block. The entrance rooms were large with pillars interspersed with stone benches running down the sides. Windows were high up, and at one end a marble table had impressive statues of Jupiter and Mars on it. Clara would wait at the entrance and meet Viviana a few yards down the road. Together they would carry the bags of laundry back to their two rooms in the block where twenty others also lived, about half a mile away from the harbour. The roads at the top of the hill where the generals and the nobles lived were firmer than the stony tracks that led down the hill into the town. As they carried the bags downhill, the filth and sewage would collect into static pools and they had to be careful not to drop the bags into them.

For Viviana and Columba, the daily routine of clothes washing meant first soaking the tunics and stoles in large tubs of water which Clara would organise usually before sunrise. It would be on a rough piece of ground close to where they lived in the tiered block called an *insulae*. She would collect the clothes to be washed from the houses on the previous evening and lay them out indoors ready for the next day.

When it came to cleaning the items, it was the custom to use urine. Columba enjoyed urinating on the cloth even though Clara kept asking him to use a bucket which could be poured over it more evenly. When it came to treading and stamping on the cloth, Viviana was very conscientious whilst Columba was much less enthusiastic.

While she worked, Viviana would often muse about her life. Why had her mother become a Christian? What was this bright hope she enjoyed which shone through the cascade of troubles which came along every day? How did she know that the story of Christ's death and resurrection was true? What did she think of her husband going to war? And what did she feel when he came back injured? She amused herself with the thought of telling Columba that if their father had not returned home injured from the fighting, for a brief period, Columba would not have been born.

Columba was already more athletic and stronger than most of the other boys around his age. His eyes were dark and fiery. His temper was easily triggered and he loved winning all the races and competitions that took place on the rough, uneven ground nearby. Columba was always keen to hear stories of battles which one or two of the older men who sat outside their houses would relate. For amusement he would find sticks which he would sharpen and then kill the rats which lived in the rubbish and sewage. First, he would find stones big enough to stun the rats and then spear them through.

He knew his sister would not have satisfactory answers to his questions. How many battles had his father won? How many barbarians had he killed with his own hands? Was he honoured by Diocletian? What did his armour look like? Was he given a horse? How did he die? And what were his last words? Most importantly, did he want Columba to follow in his footsteps? He would visualise his mother's last moments – who would he rather be, the soldier spearing his mother, or his mother being speared? He did not have to think; the question answered itself.

He would also go on long walks and ponder. *How can the God of the Christians protect us when my mother was left to be torn apart by the dogs and speared to death? Why did Jupiter win the battle and let my father die? Why is Viviana praying all the time? Why does she never question anything? If she is honouring my mother, she is also dishonouring my father. Which God is she displeasing the most?*

As the weeks went by Columba gradually found his bearings as he walked further and further. He would see where the potters, jewellers and bread-makers worked. The higher up he went, he saw more closely where the merchants lived and the edge of a huge army encampment, which was like a city in itself. Back in the town in among the bars and the public baths were also the temples to the Roman pagan gods.

On one of his walks, Columba saw some smoke coming over a ridge from the outskirts of town. He went a little further and found three or four pottery and iron-smelting workshops nestled into the hillside. Piles of bricks were stacked up ready for transport, but under cover and partly obscured were some statues of Jupiter and what looked like some other gods. Later Columba learned that the statues were being prepared for the houses of the wealthy, the temples in the town and the emperor's palace itself. Down below a road emerged and Columba could see the carts carrying away the earthenware, shields and knives; on one was a very large statue. He looked down the road and worked out that it bent round towards the harbour. Then a long way away he could see heavily laden carts coming up from the opposite direction.

Columba sought out where the temples to the gods were in the town and he listened to the priests or *Augures* interpreting the patterns of flight of birds from outside the entrances. There were others, *Haruspices,* who found meaning in the entrails of sacrificed animals. The temples had more than a single god inside them and

Columba wondered how they were connected. One day a *Haruspice* saw him peering in: 'What do you want?'

Columba was taken aback. Unaware of his own naivety, he said, 'How do the gods know each other?'

The *Haruspice* beckoned him inside and told him to wait. After a few moments he returned. 'I will need a sign from the gods before I say anything. Bring a young goat here and sacrifice it to the gods. I will see from its entrails what I must say and not say.'

Columba saw the look of disdain the *Haruspice* gave him. Unable to hide his youth, he confidently blurted out a reassurance. 'I will bring the goat here at first light and slay it myself.'

The *Haruspice* almost smiled and turned away. Columba went home but got up stealthily around 2 a.m., taking one of Clara's knives and a length of rope with him. The night was clear and stars shone through the canopy as he made his way to a small hillside farm. He had taken some carrots and cabbage from Clara's store and quietly dropped them in the ramshackle enclosure where a few goats ambled around. While they were eating, he led one of the younger goats out of the pen, putting a rope loosely round its neck. He arrived at the temple as the first shafts of dawn emerged. As he entered the temple with the goat, he saw the *Haruspice* asleep on the floor. He slowly prodded him and looked pleased with himself when the priest saw the goat. As they emerged from the temple onto the open ground, Columba stunned the animal, using a brick. He took out the knife and slit the goat's throat.

The *Haruspice* dispassionately instructed Columba to disembowel the goat and show him the intestines and liver. Columba's arms and legs were covered in blood as he duly obliged. The *Haruspice* looked up and began to speak. Columba had difficulty following the torrent that flowed. He could not make head nor tail of some of it: Jupiter was a husband to his sister? The three brothers and the sister overthrew their father. Jupiter swallowed a pregnant woman . . . ? The unborn child wanted to overthrow Jupiter . . .

Columba's eyes grew wider as he digested the tales of incest, the swallowing of children and displacement of parents. 'Yes, tell me more,' he urged.

The *Haruspice* waited for a moment and asked, 'Do you want to know how Rome was born?' Columba nodded vigorously. The Haruspice went on telling the most complicated of stories but Columba learned that Romulus and Remus argued where Rome should be placed, and Romulus murdered Remus to win the argument. And then when Rome was established, Romulus arranged for a celebration with a neighbouring tribe, but halfway through gave orders for the young women to be carried off as wives for the men of Rome, and so the next generation emerged.

The *Haruspice* continued on talking about many gods – among which were gods of fertility, nature, virility, aggression, prostitution, wine, water, earthquakes, agriculture, slaves and domestic life. After an hour or so, the *Haruspice* went inside for some wood; he came out and set fire to the goat, saying prayers as it burned down into ashes. He looked up, saying, 'You wanted to know how the gods know each other, didn't you? Now you know.'

Columba walked to the harbour and did his best to wash away the blood. Some of the spots remained and his tunic was marked. In among it all he remembered that Romulus had murdered Remus, his brother . . . that was the kind of act he knew he was capable of.

Columba came home later in the morning, replaced the knife and rope, put on a different tunic and carried on with the daily laundry tasks as if nothing out of the ordinary had happened. The normal routine continued, but what he had learned from the *Haruspice* overwhelmed him. He thought to himself, *Why should I not speak out? I am a man now, not a boy.*

The next morning, Viviana asked Columba to help her move a heavy tub full of clothes. He grudgingly helped and then dropped the tub rather than put it down. It almost fell on Viviana's foot. Columba's anger spilled over, taking Viviana unawares.

'What sort of God lets Jupiter kill our father and our mother die in the amphitheatre? What do you know about the gods? How do you know whether they have battles with each other or not? You do *not*, Viviana, do you? Do you know why our father died?'

Viviana stared in amazement as Columba blamed their mother for their father's death. The god Jupiter had foreseen that Phyllis would become a Christian and so had brought about the death of their father. Now Viviana received the brunt of Columba's anger and his taunts about how many battles the Christian God had won. Once the Christian God had won battles for the empire, she could worship her God freely!

While he was still speaking, Viviana walked away slowly and Columba saw red. When she turned round, he hit her hard across the face and she fell to the ground. Columba left her as she crouched in a corner behind their building. Thoughts came rushing into her mind and tears of shock rolled down her cheeks. She could see Columba betraying her; she could see herself being devoured by wild animals and Columba smiling.

Clara had heard the argument. She stopped drying the laundry and came alongside Viviana. Viviana turned her head and they embraced; their tears mingled. They eventually went inside and Clara made a pottage into which some bread and cheese could be dipped. As they were sitting down to eat, Clara began to give thanks for the food. She halted for a moment when Columba came in, but carried on. Columba started eating before Clara finished praying; his eyes were defiant and he pushed the plate away when he had finished.

Chapter Four
Two Different Pathways

Viviana was shaking; she had been to a believer's house in the middle of the night. As they prayed silently, she felt reassured while she was there, but on the way home in the half-light of dawn she felt completely different. Thoughts of deliberately ending her life crept into her mind and she did not know how to deal with them. Should she listen to them or were they sent by an evil force? When Jesus was tempted, he was asked to throw himself off the 'highest point of the temple'[9] to demonstrate the power of the angels to hold him; should she do the same or should she refrain from making a dare with God? Was Columba right? Was she interfering in battles between the gods in a way she had no right to?

She was descending further into misery as she walked quickly; with no sleep she would soon be spending another day with Clara treading on the tunics of the wealthy nobles. Furtively glancing all the time, she came to a halt near a clump of trees. Resting for a moment, a spark of hope came into her soul: St Paul had written something about God working through people when they were weak[10] – Christ himself lived and died that message. What did that mean?

Why is weakness strength? Why do we have to wait for God when he does nothing? Why do evil men prevail? What are women for? Is it worth trying to be understood? What if no one is interested? Are some of us just there to be used by others to make them feel good? Is there no such thing as . . . ?

Words dried up but she could still see two pathways.

---

9. Matthew 4:5.
10. 2 Corinthians 12:9.

Columba only opens his soul to the gods who will give him power. But I don't want power – my soul yearns for someone who hears and understands. If that is God, then he will not be able to understand unless he has suffered like me; a God who does not suffer is a God who cannot understand me. I want a God who I can tell I feel like killing myself. I want to know a God who has felt like that himself. Where is that God? God, can you hear me when I think of doing the worst?

A few days later, Viviana went back to the believer's house. She could not find the courage to tell them what she had found in her heart after the last visit – admitting she had felt like killing herself would be like saying that her faith was too weak; it would be *her* fault. The other believers were so self-assured and seemed to welcome troubles as a means of demonstrating their belief. She could not do that.

Very quietly a reading was shared from Mark's Gospel about Jesus in the garden of Gethsemane. Jesus 'began to be deeply distressed and troubled. "My soul is overwhelmed with sorrow to the point of death," he said to them . . . Going a little farther, he fell to the ground and prayed that if possible the hour might pass from him. "*Abba*, Father," he said, "everything is possible for you. Take this cup from me. Yet not what I will, but what you will."[11]

While the other believers seemed to find strength in encouraging one another to face adversity and persecution, Viviana was struck as to why Jesus had said what he *actually* felt. And openly – the other disciples must have witnessed it.

Viviana wondered if she had any living faith at all. Was it just a tribal connection with others, all of whom were braver than her? She knew she had something precious, but it seemed to be different to what the other believers valued the most. More than a God who had suffered, she needed a God who would truly suffer with her now. For

---

11. Mark 14:32-36.

that God had to be alive – alive enough to suffer? She felt complete disdain for Columba's quest for power, but strangely enough she also felt distant from the other Christians around her. She was alone except for Clara.

One morning Columba went off from home. His physical absence was no longer unusual, but the most he ever stayed away from home was around two days as hunger would drive him back. Columba was very strong, tall and wily, but it was his fierce dark eyes that would make people hesitate for a moment when they caught his stare. He spent a great deal of time daydreaming:

When I become the emperor, Viviana and Clara will realise how foolish they have been to ignore my strength. Am I a God? I am strong, fearless and there is nothing that will stop me from killing men, women and children if I have to – in fact, it will be a pleasure in my search for glory. That is the power I have over others – a power which ordinary people are not given. My father's bravery and my mother's stubbornness have made me a warrior king. Viviana is of a different kind; she is scared of hurting people and cares about people's feelings. I am not one of them; I will be a god myself. One day I will have my own coinage with my head on it; it will say this:

'The god, Columba, cherished by the gods'

Once I can murder on behalf of an emperor, it would not be too much more of a step to murder an emperor himself – for that has been the story behind some of the greatest of our leaders; evil is conquered by evil.

Over the months, Columba had become friendly with some soldiers who belonged to Severus, the Caesar who was second-in-command to the Eastern emperor, Galerius. Columba imbibed their stories and told himself his first step would be to become a commander, a legate, of a 5,000-strong legion. One of the young men he talked to a lot was Beatus. One night Beatus left the camp and met Columba in a deserted place. They talked till the early hours of the morning. Columba had made out to him that he was setting off for the Bosphorus where supply ships would leave for Rome. He led Beatus to believe that they would meet in Rome in six months' time from where they could judge whether Severus or Maxentius was most likely to win the battle for supremacy. They, of course, would join the stronger side.

In fact, Columba had already made his mind up not to go, and returned home. He had realised that without being able to read and write he could be easily deceived by those who could. He kept his thoughts to himself.

I want to be like the god Fraus, Orcus' daughter – until, one day, like her I overcome my own kin. Like her, my face is human but my body is like a snake with a scorpion's sting. I cannot truly learn the art of deception until I can deceive those closest to me. Rome must wait a short while.

Chapter Five
Towards Alexandria

Columba, chameleon-like, began to work regularly, fetching the laundry and laying it out and then returning it to the nobleman's house under Clara's direction. Clara and Viviana, even though they knew Columba had ulterior motives, nevertheless took respite from it. The three of them would eat in silence as the evening light faded. Viviana might steal a look at Columba but learn nothing from it. His face could conceal his inner thoughts like a fortress and his eyes, even though they were open, were closed in every other sense. How would he react to anything he might think intrusive? Where had he buried all his pent-up anger? When next would it burst out against her and Clara?

One evening he suddenly looked up and asked Viviana to recite part of Paul's letter to the Ephesians. 'I want to hear anything St Paul wrote to the Christians at Ephesus,' he said, somewhat coldly.

Viviana was completely taken aback but she did not change her expression. She took three more mouthfuls and then looked up. It was word perfect:

> Do not let any unwholesome talk come out of your mouths, but only what is helpful for building others up according to their needs, that it may benefit those who listen. And do not grieve the Holy Spirit of God, with whom you were sealed for the day of redemption. Get rid of all bitterness, rage and anger, brawling and slander, along with every form of malice. Be kind and compassionate to one another, forgiving each other, just as in Christ God forgave you.[12]

---

12. Ephesians 4:29-32.

Clara looked down as she gathered up the bowls. Columba said 'Thank you' to Viviana and went out, coming back a few hours later to sleep before getting up early to once again work on the dirty laundry. About once a week he would ask Viviana to recite a passage from Scripture – he seemed particularly interested in the Second Coming when the world would be judged.

One day he arrived home with a reed pen, parchment and pigmented ink. He asked Viviana to write down some words which she had recited and he began to copy them. Clara had gained a basic understanding of *Koine* Greek which she needed for her laundry business and she had passed this knowledge on to Viviana. Slowly Viviana wrote out a passage from memory from Paul's first letter in *Koine* Greek to the Corinthians.

And so it was with me, brothers and sisters. When I came to you, I did not come with eloquence or human wisdom as I proclaimed to you the testimony about God. For I resolved to know nothing while I was with you except Jesus Christ and him crucified. I came to you in weakness with great fear and trembling. My message and my preaching were not with wise and persuasive words, but with a demonstration of the Spirit's power, so that your faith might not rest on human wisdom, but on God's power.[13]

The words which Columba chose to learn to copy were these:

Wisdom
Resolved
Nothing

---

13. 1 Corinthians 2:1-5.

Except
Fear
Demonstration
Power

Viviana and Clara both wanted to know where he had obtained the parchment, pen and ink but again thought better of asking. Viviana waited till Columba had gone out and began to voice her fears. 'We know there is something wrong. I have no idea what he is planning, but we can only think that his interest in our faith is false, isn't it? He is biding his time for something. And he is using us to learn to read and write...'

They both knew what the brothers and sisters would say. It would be something around simply trusting and waiting. The dilemma began to emerge. Should they wait for God to resolve the situation, perhaps by praying all the time for Columba, or should they take the matter into their own hands and get him to leave the house? As Viviana sat there, she was entirely taken aback by the fact of her entertaining a wild thought: that of poisoning her brother. Was this someone else – another person who she did not know? Indeed, it was her; she realised how desperate she was.

'I have just thought of something, but I cannot...' she whispered.

Sitting in silence for a while, Viviana then told Clara what had crossed her mind. Clara shook her head and Viviana knew, tempting as it was, she did not want to be like him; then she would no longer be able to live with herself. Viviana took a long pause and, holding her head in her hands, she said, 'I have to leave and take him on the first step of his journey to Rome. I think he wants to learn more about the empire, so I might try to go to Alexandria with him. I have to find a way to persuade him.'

Viviana tried to reassure Clara that she would find two other workers. She said she would rather die than let Columba hurt or even kill Clara – her feelings were a mixture of hate and guilt towards him; she didn't even feel she knew who she was. She wanted God to help her. Clara looked up and met Viviana's eyes.

'You are such a beautiful flower, that you would even think of protecting me from Columba's fury. I love you, Viviana. I do not want you to leave me, Viviana, and if you do go, I am fearful of what Columba might do; how do you know he won't abandon you, or even worse? You would be putting yourself into great danger.'

After a while they could talk and think no more – they went to sleep. Over the next few days, they talked of little else when Columba was out.

When Clara was outside, Viviana surprised Columba.

'Do you think that Severus will defeat Maxentius in Rome?'

Columba thought for a moment, wondering how Viviana knew a battle was looming.

'Why should I be concerned?' he said, nonchalantly.

'Because you are waiting for a chance to climb the ladder in the Roman army, and you want to know how the land lies in Rome,' said Viviana instantly. 'You want to become one of the gods, but they can read and write and you cannot.' She could barely contain her suppressed anger with him, her body moving around as she spoke. Columba pretended to dismiss it – he thought of hitting her to keep her quiet but that did not satisfy him. She continued on: 'If you want to conquer the empire, you are wasting your time here. Travel with me to Alexandria and find out how far the empire stretches – we will then see how mighty and clever you are. From there you can go on to Rome.'

Columba did not relax his implacable façade. 'Why would you leave Clara? She is like a mother to you?'

'Clara has given us a home; you have taken it for granted – I have not. I do not want her troubled by your ambitions. It is better we go. The church in Alexandria will give us shelter and from there you can sail to Naples and travel on to Rome as you wish; unless, of course,' she said, and added coolly, 'you become a bishop. Of course I will return, but you will only become more and more frustrated here and I do not want that for Clara.'

Columba left without another word. He went out to the edge of town, found a young goat and went back to the temple to the same *Haruspic.* He explained that he was thinking of travelling to Alexandria. They slaughtered the goat as before and Columba listened intently to the priest's instructions. After cleaning the goat's liver, Columba could see the shape of it; it was put to one side. The goat was set alight.

The *Haruspic* looked through the flames at Columba and said, 'When the flames have died down and the fire is smouldering, throw the liver into the air and take a journey within the next three months in whichever direction the cleft is pointing towards.'

He walked off without another word. Columba sat and watched the flames and then carried out the priest's instructions. He threw the goat's liver into the air and the cleft landed, pointing to the left of the harbour. Columba was not certain but thought it could be in the direction of the Mediterranean coast towards Alexandria.

Clara was down at the waterside as one of the ships bringing grain from Alexandria was unloading its cargo onto what seemed like hundreds of carts, all with toiling slaves and mules bearing loads up the hill. She was surrounded by a cacophony of orders, shouting and braying as she found her way up the gangplank. One of the households they did the laundry for were grain merchants. They had given their consent to Columba and Viviana travelling on board; all Clara had to do was mention that to the captain.

A few minutes later she came back down, followed by two slaves carrying four very large bags of clothing and bedding. Clara had offered to do the captain's laundry before the ship left. After climbing up the hill, the laundry was immediately soaked, trodden in with urine and put out to dry.

When Columba returned home, Clara spoke to him firmly.

'The ship is setting off for Alexandria in three days for another consignment of grain. The captain has agreed to take you both – together with Viviana you will do his laundry as payment, and also help with the cooking. For Viviana's sake I have told the captain that you and she are man and wife – it is the only way that she will be protected from the other men if you *pretend*, but you must not violate her.'

Columba simply nodded. And then he added, 'Clara, when I return, I will be a commander in the Roman army. Viviana wants me to leave because she cares for you, not me, but one day I will come back. Who will do your laundry now?'

Clara replied, 'I have already found two young women from a family I know.'

Nothing more was said. Columba wondered if he was being trapped into something more sinister by his aunt and sister and decided to consult the gods again: he stole another young goat and went back to the temple. This time the cleft in the goat's liver pointed much more in the direction of Gaul, and so Columba sought out the *Haruspic* for guidance once more: 'Follow your instincts and listen to the gods –

when you are faced with a choice, remember the signs you have been given...'

Columba, not knowing what to do, knelt down by the burnt carcass and prayed: 'I will sacrifice to you, Neptune. In your temple at Rome, I will sacrifice a bull in gratitude – I promise you, O god of the sea, that I will repay you for your good fortune...'

Columba knew he would have to make up his own mind. Knowing that his journey was just at the beginning he would, for the moment, leave his destiny in the hands of the gods. He began to think that the cleft pointing in the direction of Gaul may have a hidden meaning for him. Perhaps it was a warning that Viviana was not as innocent and kind as she made herself out to be.

Three days later they were down at the harbour. Clara and Viviana looked at each other. Clara could not find any words. They embraced. Would they see one another again? How long would it be? The storm clouds separated for a momentary shaft of sunlight. Columba just looked at Clara, turned round and walked onto the ship, carrying the captain's laundry.

It was only a month or so before the sea and weather conditions would prohibit sailing across the Mediterranean. The ship was lighter now the grain from Egypt had been unloaded – it would return with one more consignment before the winter. The 140 slaves would eat, live and row below deck while the twenty or so crew would watch, cajole and whip them to make sure the ship went as fast as it could. The slaves' only view of the open sea would be when they relieved themselves through an iron grate into the sea; they would wipe themselves with a rope which would then be dropped back into the water. They were allowed a few hours' sleep and would curl up on the floor before getting back to pulling on the oars. The ship had set out from Alexandria with 150 slaves but ten of them had died on the way and were thrown overboard to their final resting place.

The crew slept in the hold or on deck under canvas, depending on the weather conditions. Viviana and Columba worked on deck most of the time with makeshift tubs for washing and large pots for preparing the porridge, soups and fish on board. Meticulous care was taken to ensure that the wood-burning stoves heating the pots were as self-contained as possible.

When the wind was in the forward direction the oarsmen were given a lighter load, and for a few days the ship made good progress. When conditions worsened, the ship would head for shelter. For navigation, the sun was used by day and the stars, when they were visible, at night. A week into the journey, blustery head winds took hold, slowing progress down, so the captain decided to head for the coastal town of Seleucia near Antioch – two of the oarsmen died on the way.

At night, Viviana and Columba would lie side by side. Viviana was not sure how to feel with Columba so close. She never felt relaxed enough to fall into a deep sleep. On the first night she whispered to him, 'Columba, if you force yourself on me, I will scream – the crew will turn on you because they will want me, so beware.'

She could see he was taken aback by her words. She realised that when Columba sensed that a crew member was close by at night, he would roll over onto her. She began to feel more and more troubled by his so-called 'acting' and felt that he would have no hesitation in violating her had she not threatened to reveal that they were brother and sister. She prayed fervently for help and more so after one of the crew remarked that they resembled each other. She wished she could talk with Clara, and began to feel increasingly desperate. She made up her mind that she would have to try to find shelter in Antioch.

When the boat came into Seleucia, they both went ashore. Columba was looking for somewhere to have a drink in a crowded square when Viviana took her chance and ran away towards Antioch. It took many hours to walk the fifteen miles as she followed the river Orantes. Finally, she discovered a city with a huge amphitheatre and a large temple. It was the middle of the night and the city rose upwards onto a hillside, with the wealthier houses being higher up, just as they were in her home town of Nicomedia. The filth and rancid water trickled down the pathways and narrow streets in-between the mud-built houses in the same way. The believers in Nicomedia had given her the names of Christians in various places but she did not have one in Antioch, as she had thought the ship would not stop near there. However, she did remember the names of some of the Christians in Antioch the believers in Nicomedia had prayed for.

Once Columba realised that Viviana had disappeared, he went looking for her. After a few hours he returned to the boat, telling the captain that she must have been kidnapped. He said he would search for her again the next day; if he could not find her, he would continue on the journey, hopefully collecting her on the way back. The captain thought it strange that Columba was not more concerned, but did not care as he needed his help on board. Columba knew he would have to work twice as hard but at least he could pursue his ambitions without the encumbrance of his sister.

After two days the weather abated and the ship sailed for Alexandria without Viviana.

PART 2

The Persecution Ends

Chapter Six
Marriage: The Year 313 in Antioch

Once the 'Edict of Milan' in 313 was passed, many more Christians emerged than even the believers themselves had anticipated. Some, of course, were not genuinely 'converted' but had heard that both emperors were now sympathetic towards the Church.

Church leaders in Antioch talked of building a cathedral just offshore where the imperial palace once stood on a small island. For the moment, the faithful met in various believers' houses but the hierarchy of the bishop, elders and deacons was now much more visible and active across all the groups in the city. The Church's authority structure was starting to fall into place.

Eight years had passed since Viviana had run away from Columba into those dark streets and to Antioch, panicking wildly. Now, finally, she was able to pen a letter to Clara. It would be sent through one of the Church leaders who would travel to visit some of the churches in Asia Minor; Christians were no longer hiding from the authorities.

My dear Clara

My heart is overflowing with memories and as I write this letter, it is as if we are standing side by side treading the laundry together. I do not know where to begin. I pray with all my heart that you receive this and that somehow you are able to send news back to me. It has been agonising to wait all this time but at last I can write to you.

At last the persecutions are over. Emperors Constantine and Licinius have granted what they call 'The Edict of Milan'. Licinius was one of the chief persecutors so I can only think he has stopped because Emperor Constantine thinks the God of the Christians may be the greatest God after all. I thought he worshipped Apollo but if all gods are worshipped, I suppose none of them are left out – even if they are jealous of each other?

I did not sail all the way to Alexandria. Although the storm in Galilee terrified the disciples, the bad weather saved me from Columba. I really thought he would try to be a proper husband and if the ship had not had to change course for Seleucia, I think he would have ended up raping me. Some of the sailors did not think that we were husband and wife, and I am sure he saw that as a challenge to his manhood. I ran away desperately, hoping to find a believer in Antioch, fifteen miles up the river; I could remember the believers in Nicomedia praying for them and one or two of the names came back to me.

Columba must have come looking for me; I walked for many hours into the night so he would not find me. Early in the morning a passing woman threw me a scrap of bread. I went to the local market and asked if anyone knew the names, and by a miracle I found one of them. I spoke about my mother and mentioned the names of the believers in Nicomedia and they took me in. Thank God for their mercy.

It is a long story but Simon, the tentmaker, is married to Lydia and they have two sons, Ethan and Lucas. I sleep in one small corner of the large room. I work to sew up the tents which the Roman army buy. Everyone works in the small workshop. Simon and Lydia are gentle and humble – they have no pretentions. They are very spiritual people without being proud. They have saved my life. The church is getting larger and there is much joy now that worship can take place openly. I am not as full of joy as I should be; the shadows of my life never seem to completely go away – the death of my mother and father, Columba's hatefulness and life without you – they are the things I cannot change.

Clara, you saved our lives for which I will be forever grateful. Columba, as you know, can only think of himself: he may have reached Alexandria and it was always in his mind to go to Rome – he is probably a general in the army. I pray earnestly that you also have a better life now. Oh, how I long to hear from you. I dream of seeing you.

Clara, my heart will always be for you and I would love to know that you are safe. I cannot write more as we do not have much papyrus, and the traveller has many letters to carry with him.

My love to you in the grace of God.

Viviana

In the rush of excitement of being able to write to Clara, Viviana had momentarily put aside what those eight years of hiding and daily toil had done to her, but the shadows she spoke about in her letter to Clara were there. Even with the overwhelming kindness of Simon and Lydia, she had had many moments of inner bleakness.

Why do I feel like this? I have no right to be discontent – but where is my life going? I love it when the fellowship of believers sing and praise together but everyone is so triumphant. There is never any room for anything else. They tell us our troubles should be welcomed as 'gifts', yes, 'gifts' – a chance to exercise faith. I wish I could say 'yes' but I can't.

Simon and Lydia took me in as if I was their own, but what will happen when they die? Will I have to rely on someone else's mercy? Ethan and Lucas will marry their betrothed soon, and the dowries will have to be paid. They keep talking about the Lord's return but it is more than 250 years since he died and rose again. If I were to say anything, the teachers would no doubt tell me to have more faith – I cannot even pray, for when I pray it is not God who is 'listening', it is the elders of the church.

The other women never admit to any doubt. They are always so sure that God will do this or that – they have prayed and so it must be? They submit to their husbands, and even Ethan and Lucas' betrothed do, so I cannot say anything and I don't. They all talk about me as gentle and kind, but my lips are sealed. I cannot, nor do I want to forget the kindness of this Christian family. In Columba's world I would have just been a sex slave. So, what is the matter with me? Am I expecting too much? At least my life has not been torn apart like my poor mother's.

God must be angry with me for being so ungrateful. I must try to remember the good things. Am I so sinful that when I have been saved from Columba's world I still feel empty? Stop, stop – there is food to prepare.

The light was fading as Lydia and Viviana cleared away after the evening meal. Ethan and Lucas had gone back to the workshop as Simon waited for the visit. When Silas, one of the elders arrived, Lydia and Viviana stayed in the kitchen.

Simon offered him a seat, slightly bowing his head as Silas began to speak. Now the persecution was over, the Church had a mission – there had been a famous Bishop of Antioch who, when he was taken to Rome to be martyred, wrote to all the churches, telling them to heed the instructions of the elders and deacons. Silas referred to the apostle Paul's letter to Timothy, which talked about single women in the Church. The letter said that the Church should confine itself to looking after widows of sixty years and over and that younger widows should marry.[14] Although Viviana was not a widow, Silas made it clear that because Simon and Lydia had taken her in as one of their

---

14. 1 Timothy 5:9-11.

own, she should be treated as their daughter. Simon looked at Silas knowing there was more to come.

'Quite simply, Viviana should marry for she is too young for the church to look after her, should anything happen to you. As elders we see it as our responsibility to make sure the church's giving is channelled in the way the apostle intended.'

Silas carried on pointing out the temptations which Viviana would be open to once Simon and Lydia had died. The elders had a concrete proposal which Simon was anticipating.

'Brother John, as you know, has a son, Benedict, who is devoted to the Lord. He has preached from the apostle Paul's letter to the Romans with great authority and understanding. We want him to become a deacon and for that it would best for him to marry. He is the same age as Viviana and now the persecution has ended, he himself wants to marry into the fellowship in order to honour the Lord. Is that acceptable to you, Simon?'

Simon nodded submissively, but he had many questions and concerns which he could not voice; later on, he would submit them to the Lord in prayer. The greatest of these fears was not to do with Benedict but his father, John, who was fierce in his defence of the gospel but equally fierce in his attitude towards those who dissented. Simon wondered what would befall Viviana if she were to voice any sympathies towards people John would classify as disloyal. He had once heard Viviana praying in a whisper and that had been enough to give him an insight into the workings of her mind. He sensed that underneath her complicity she was a free spirit.

While this conversation was taking place in the main room, Lydia and Viviana were washing the dishes in the kitchen. Viviana asked Lydia what she thought the reason for Silas' visit was.

'The elders want all young women in the church to marry, Viviana – but I do not know what he will say to Simon.'

Lydia tried to keep her own emotions under control, for she loved Viviana. She could see that Viviana was perturbed by what she had just said. She tried to reassure her. 'We can only trust the Lord. The apostle Paul taught that the Church is the bride of Christ. We have to hold on and believe that the Lord will provide us with husbands who care for us as Christ cares for the Church.[15] I am blessed with Simon.'

Viviana winced as she thought of some of the marriages in the church. She knew of one elder who had married one of his slaves. His now wife had a reputation of ordering her former fellow slaves to be beaten when they did not perform their duties adequately.

Viviana carried on with the dishes.

The two families met in Silas' house: Simon, Lydia and Viviana sat on a wooden bench, with John and Benedict sitting on a box on the other side of the room. Silas sat in the middle on a seat called a curule; it had wooden legs with some carved patterns around the frame of the seat which was covered with reddish woollen material and stuffed with feathers. He opened in prayer.

'Lord God, we give our heartfelt thanks for your mercy on us. Guide and direct us as we seek to witness to our new life in the risen Christ, your eternal Son. May we follow your will for our lives and keep the faith, whatever lies before us. Thank you for the gift of marriage for Benedict and Viviana. As we submit to you, O Lord, may Viviana also submit to the will of her husband as he, in turn, loves her just as you love the Church.'

Silas began by asking John and Simon if they were in accordance with the wishes of the elders. John looked at Silas directly without

---

15. Ephesians 5:25.

glancing at Simon and Lydia, confirming that he believed it was the Lord's will.

Lydia very gently nudged Simon; he realised that he needed to say that he also believed it was the Lord's will but added this: 'Yes, but both Benedict and Viviana must also be in accord with this union.'

Silas turned to them both to ask if they had any reason why the wishes of both families and the elders should be opposed. Benedict said that he wanted the marriage to proceed. Viviana nodded in tacit agreement without revealing any of her true feelings.

Benedict is a stranger to me. His father believes in strict discipline. I have heard him preach at church. Am I really marrying Benedict, or is he just his father's puppet? Where is the mother? Why is there no word of her? Will I see Simon and Lydia? I am sure they will try to have complete control over me . . .

They were given a few minutes to introduce themselves to each other, while John and Simon stood with Silas, quietly discussing the arrangements for the wedding. John hardly engaged with Simon except when discussing the prospective date for the ceremony.

When Simon, Lydia and Viviana returned home, Lydia looked at Viviana as if to ask what she thought of Benedict. Viviana smiled at her, for she could not bring herself to upset Lydia. After a while she said, 'All will be well; I need to trust the Lord. Benedict says his mother left the home many years ago but his father will not permit any mention of it.'

Lydia nodded, wondering how Viviana would cope with the extra demands that would be placed on her; she would be a wife to Benedict, but also a daughter-in-law to John. She gently placed her hand on Viviana's forearm and said, 'May the Lord guide you and keep you. We will pray for you every day.'

In her heart, Lydia felt a strange kind of loss. Viviana's gentle presence in her life had brought with it a sense of togetherness which was about to disappear. Lydia knew Simon felt the same. They had taken her in and she had become part of the family, but now they had been instructed by the church to release her. She knew that seeing Viviana at church would not provide an opportunity for any kind of honest exchange, as she would be under her husband's authority. They could only do what they always did, accept their fate and trust God that they would get through it.

Chapter Seven
Divided Loyalties

Viviana's eyes were wide open for several hours before a half-sleep briefly took over. She had been married for six months and, as she had suspected, Benedict was completely dominated by his father. There were also other difficulties. As she lay there with Benedict by her side, she went over once again what she had overheard six weeks before: 'Is she with child, Benedict? It is a simple enough question, isn't it?'

Benedict drew breath. 'I do not know, Father. Father, I do not know how to consummate the marriage! I have read the story of Genesis over and over, but I do not know what a man should do . . .'

Silence had followed and Viviana had stood completely still in the hallway. She could not see the tears rolling down Benedict's face. She heard John's sigh. When Benedict showed vulnerability, John instantly recoiled. 'Crying will not help, Benedict. You cannot be a true husband unless the marriage is consummated. If the marriage is not, it will then have to be annulled and you will have to step down from being a deacon.'

Viviana felt she should withdraw in case she was heard, but Benedict and his father carried on. John was frustrated with Benedict's inability to consummate the marriage, but thought back for a moment to his own clumsy attempts many years before. He was now much more concerned for his own reputation in the church than for Benedict and Viviana themselves.

'You will bring shame on this house. Have we not had enough disgrace through your mother's unfaithfulness?' He drew himself together and then put his hand on his son's shoulder, firmly. 'Let us pray. Father God, we pray that you will enable Benedict and Viviana to fulfil your creation plan for all. We pray that they will be fruitful and bear children who can be schooled in the faith and become disciples of our Lord and Saviour. Amen.'

John looked at Benedict and said, 'Read the Song of Solomon in the Scriptures and then God will guide you.'

Over the next few days Viviana noticed Benedict reading the Scriptures, but it was to no avail. She began to reflect on a choice which she had not ever suspected she would be given.

Now I have a chance to decide for myself. I could make it public that the marriage has not been made whole. I could return to Simon and Lydia, but then they would definitely be under pressure to find me another husband – the church wants me to marry. But if the church seeks out someone, it could be anyone – gentle, like Benedict, or harsh, like his father, or even worse, someone like Columba. I know Benedict now, although I wish he could stand up for himself. Do I want to leave Benedict for him to suffer alone at his father's hands? No, I would rather stay here, even though I cannot say what feelings I have for him. I have some but I do not know how deep they are. Perhaps there is no choice to be made after all?

Viviana decided to talk with Benedict to help him understand what he needed to do to consummate the marriage, and gradually he became more confident in their intimate moments. Without any real experience to fall back on, she had found an opportunity to speak with Lydia very briefly after church one Sunday.

A few months later she told him that she was with child. Viviana saw that Benedict was overcome with emotion and hugged him as tears of joy flowed down their cheeks.

'What did he say?' Viviana asked Benedict after he told his father.

'He just looked up for a moment and then said: "Good. Now leave me and attend to the church finances – I have a sermon to prepare."'

They looked at each other and after a second or two, just laughed.

The services held on a Sunday lasted for several hours, with only those who had been baptised staying for the Eucharist. There were several preachers, interspersed with prayers and long Scripture readings. Some of the liturgy was sung with very plain tunes, as the leaders did not want any resemblance to the excessive way passions could be aroused in pagan worship with music and dancing. The church building had been restored and many new people had now started to come.

John stood up to preach the sermon he had been preparing when Benedict had told him that he and Viviana were going to have a child. He started by reading from the Scriptures where Jesus was talking to the disciples shortly before he was brought before the Pharisees:

I am the vine; you are the branches. If you remain in me and I in you, you will bear much fruit; apart from me you can do nothing. If you do not remain in me, you are like a branch that is thrown away and withers; such branches are picked up, thrown into the fire and burned. If you remain in me and my words remain in you, ask whatever you wish, and it will be done for you. This is to my Father's glory, that you bear much fruit, showing yourselves to be my disciples.[16]

John paused and looked at the congregation in a superior way.

'These are the words of our Lord. There can be no doubt, can there, that he was unequivocal about how devoted to him we should be?

---

16. John 15:5-8.

It could not be half-hearted; it could not be blown backwards and forwards by the wind, or by the changing fortunes of men, or by the whims of emperors and their so-called gods. So, what are we to say? That we can choose when to serve Christ when we want to and turn back when it gets difficult? That when we are persecuted we can deny him and when the emperor turns to Christ we can change our minds? We are not to test the Lord our God!'

As Viviana listened, she realised he was building up to naming those believers who had either worshipped the pagan gods during the time of persecution or been equivocal about standing up for Christ against the Roman authorities. He would not be doing this without a purpose – word had spread how other churches had named those who had been disloyal to the faith during the persecution. Penances had been demanded and some had been permanently excluded from churches. She tried to catch Benedict's eye but his head was bowed to the floor, as it always was when his father spoke.

Viviana heard that God could forgive anything but repentance had to be publicly demonstrated for all to see if, as John kept saying, the church was to remain pure and undefiled by sin.

John outlined how this would work in practice. For those who had signed the Roman certificate pledging worship to the emperor and his gods during the persecution, they would have to stay at the door of the church praying for forgiveness for three years before they could enter. For those who had actively helped the persecuting Roman authorities in any way which was deemed by the elders to be a denial of faith, they would not be allowed to enter the church for a year and once that was completed it would be for the judgement of the elders as to when they could take the Eucharistic sacrament.

John began to read out the names of those who had signed the certificate. One by one they stood up and left the church in full view of the congregation, to kneel outside where two of the elders would hear them pray for forgiveness. They would remain there until the end of the service when the rest of the congregation filed past them on their way out.

Viviana realised that Simon and Lydia could be on the list. They had been spared by the Roman soldiers in past times because of the trade they had with them. Tents were always wearing out and needing replacement. The local Roman legate had told his centurions to leave Simon's household alone as long as the tents were made on time, and they always were.

John waited to the very end before he read out their names, giving Simon a piercing look. As Simon and Lydia rose to leave, John read out this verse: 'If anyone comes to me and does not hate father and mother, wife and children, brothers and sisters – yes, even their own life – such a person cannot be my disciple.'[17]

As Simon and Lydia walked through the people, Viviana rose and walked out with them. Simon tried to encourage her to go back but she would not. Benedict looked up and saw the expression of disgust on his father's face. John continued speaking for another half an hour. When the service was over and John and Benedict came out, Viviana rose up from her kneeling position, kissed Lydia and followed John and Benedict home.

They arrived home and Viviana went to prepare food in the kitchen. The silence was laden with tension but the confrontation was not far away. John's voice was one of barely concealed rage.

'Benedict, you are the "head of the wife", as St Paul says,[18] but you have no authority over Viviana! She does as she pleases. You are disobeying God's pattern for marriage. "As the church submits to

---

17. Luke 14:26.
18. Ephesians 5:23.

Christ, so also wives should submit to their husbands in everything."[19] Do you hear, Benedict? "*In everything*"! What have you to say?'

Benedict, with his head bowed, was preparing to submit to his father when he felt what he could only later recall as an instinct pulling him in the other direction. He did not, for once, have to think about the words; they just flowed out of him. This time he looked his father straight in the eye.

'Simon and Lydia are effectively Viviana's parents, are they not? Were they involved in the marriage? Did we not go to their house with Silas the elder to seek their approval? So, if she wants to honour her "parents", who am I to tell her to disobey the sixth commandment? Viviana has helped me in ways I cannot speak of, but she has shown me gentleness; that gentleness is one of the fruits of the Holy Spirit.[20] I do not want to disrespect her and I will not. Yes, she is under my authority, but we are to love our wives 'as Christ loved the church and gave himself up for her'.[21] That is what I am doing by giving my consent for her to stand outside the church with Simon and Lydia. And Father, she is under my authority, not yours. Yes, I am your child, but in asking me to honour you,[22] you are asking me to dishonour her and I will not do that.'

Benedict looked at his father's face, frozen in shock by his son's temerity. They sat for a while and then John replied with a slight tremor in his voice.

'We are told to obey our parents so that it may go well with us and we "enjoy long life on the earth".[23] Let us see whether or not you are right. Time will tell – and also let me remind you that the key question exercising the bishops is whether those bishops who were

---

19. Ephesians 5:24.
20. Galatians 5:22-23.
21. Ephesians 5:25.
22. Ephesians 6:2.
23. Ephesians 6:3.

complicit with the Roman authorities and their pagan worship can be permitted to baptise believers.'

Benedict realised that his father had reached the real crux of what he wanted to say, that the reputation of the Church mattered more than the circumstances of individuals within it. Principles mattered more than people, for if it were the other way round, the good news of salvation would be watered down. John continued on.

'Baptism is a holy sacrament and a step that can only be taken once. It cleanses us from sin – at the most we are permitted one more sin after baptism – so the character of the bishop is crucial to the efficacy of the rite. We are not just talking about Simon and Lydia, we are there to preserve the integrity of the good news of salvation through our Lord.'

As Viviana brought in the food, none of them made eye contact. They bowed their heads as John gave thanks. Nothing further was said over the meal and afterwards John retired to his room.

Benedict sat at the table hardly believing what he had just done. Viviana squeezed Benedict's hand hard and he felt his face relax as she did so.

Once again on the following Sunday, Viviana followed Simon and Lydia out of the church, and continued to do so every week.

Chapter Eight
The Two Criminals

Benedict felt an instinctive sense of guilt after that day, but was also increasingly distressed by what was being done by the church leadership of which he was a part. He already knew from Viviana about Simon and Lydia supplying tents to the Romans, but learned that they had refused to tell the authorities the whereabouts of some who had gone into hiding. He was fully aware of how the persecution had ravaged the community of believers, but also wondered if the church was doing more than protecting the faith – was it a way of exacting revenge for disloyalty? Or was it a fear that without a harsh discipline, any sense of order in the church would be lost? He began to rehearse a resignation speech in his mind:

My dear elders and fellow deacons

You are aware that my wife has been leaving the services with her guardians, Simon and Lydia, over the past few months, and that I have not challenged her or instructed her to remain in church. I want to explain why I have not done this and therefore also explain why I no longer can be a deacon.

Simply, I do not hold with excluding all who did not publicly voice their opposition to the persecutions. I know that there are some who want lifelong excommunication for all who did not stand up for the faith publicly. However, as my father preached, I believe that anyone can be forgiven by our Lord. You will recall the two thieves on the crosses either side of our Lord. For the criminal who had a sense of right and wrong, there was no time for penance – our Lord simply said that he would be in

Paradise that very day.[24] For the other criminal who was full of anger, echoing the taunts of the crowd, he did not even want forgiveness or anything to do with the Lord.

But we are faced here and now by those two criminals, and maybe more – let me explain. The first may be a believer who was scared for his family and so burned incense and 'took the oath', but refused to give away the whereabouts of those fellow believers in hiding. The second may be a believer who also burned incense and 'took the oath', but willingly gave the authorities the names of other believers in the hope of gaining favour.

There are also those believers whom the Romans treated more leniently because of the trade they had with them – they may have handed over the Scriptures. Some of those refused to give them the names of other believers and others not. There may be others who refused to take the oath but instead paid a bribe for the certificate. Are all of these people to be branded as one, as traitors?[25] Should we not take into account the difference between genuine fear and betrayal? Are we so holy that we could not break down under such pressure?

Just as our Lord listened to the criminal, so we also should listen to each of these people and judge what the true nature of their heart is. Our Lord taught us that it is not the outward appearance that matters but the heart[26] – in the end only God sees everything.

Benedict went over his speech again and again, constantly changing it, but ending up with the reason he could no longer be a deacon, namely that the judgements of the leadership were too rigid and

---

24. Luke 23:43.
25. The original word is *traditores* from which the word 'traitor' is derived.
26. 1 Samuel 16:7.

lacked compassion. He talked it over with Viviana, who wondered if resigning in that way would cause an unbridgeable rift between Benedict and his father. Benedict agreed with her that he should share his speech with his father privately before arranging to speak to the elders. Having stood up to his father for the first time, he was determined to hold his ground. However, at night as he lay trying to sleep, his mind would run away with itself.

Will my father tell us to get out of the house? Will he go and tell the elders beforehand? Will we be estranged from him and will his grandchild never see him? What do I owe him – am I breaking the commandment by going against him?

One evening after the food had been cleared away and Viviana had retired, Benedict spoke to his father. John listened to the speech impassively and said nothing for what felt like a very long while. He then looked up.

'Benedict, do you believe that our Lord and Saviour is what the apostle John refers to as "the Word"?'[27]

'Yes, Father,' Benedict replied.

'So God the Father, God the Son and the Holy Spirit are all part of the substance of God but distinct persons?' John asked.

'Yes, Father, you know I believe that – why are you asking me?'

Benedict wondered whether he had missed something or whether he was being quietly led into a corner from which there would be no escape. His father continued.

'So if Jesus was *not* always and fully God, what would it mean for our faith, Benedict? I will tell you why I am asking these questions in a moment.'

Benedict continued on as a dutiful son. 'It would mean that God could not fully identify with human suffering and release us from

---

27. John 1:1.

wrongdoing, in which case we are no nearer God than before Christ came. Now please tell me, Father, what this has to do with my plan to speak to the elders?'

John replied, speaking very slowly, 'I do not want you to give your speech to the elders, nor do I want you to resign your post as a deacon. Instead, I want to ask them to send you and Viviana to the believers in Alexandria where there are even greater disputes going on than in Antioch about who Jesus was – many consider him to be an angel, or not fully human, or even a second-class creator of flesh and human misery. They have need of someone with your mind who can see through all those clever arguments. I will inform the elders that Simon and Lydia did not betray any believers' names to the authorities, and leave it entirely up to them if they wish to make any adjustments to the penances required of those who assisted the Romans in their persecution of the Church. I will do that for you.'

With that, John got up and left the table, leaving Benedict sitting there. Viviana came in and they decided to wait till very late, when they could hear John snoring, before discussing the conversation Benedict had had with him. Benedict listened to Viviana talking about their forthcoming child – they both wanted the child to meet John at some stage in the future rather than be completely estranged from him. The child would blame them. Benedict wondered if he should walk out with Viviana, Simon and Lydia from the service on Sunday. After thinking about it, he realised that this would amount to the same as giving the speech he had originally thought of giving. He relented.

It would be another week before the elders would meet. Benedict decided to tell his father that he would leave it to him to address the elders about the matter.

Two days later, Simon called by with a letter for Viviana. He seemed in quite a rush as he explained to Benedict what had happened. 'Now the persecutions are over, the believers have more freedom to travel and visit churches, so a letter has been left for Viviana at our house.'

Benedict thanked him for coming and gave the letter to Viviana.

Dear Viviana

It was sheer joy to hear from you. Thank God that the persecutions have ended and that you are safe. My heart is ever grateful to you for saving my life from Columba. I have news of him, but first let me say how I leapt into the air when your letter came. I have never married, but I know what love is – you took a risk with your own life just for me. Isn't that what our Lord did for us?

Life here, as everywhere, is hard, and I carry on with the laundry along with the helpers from the church. I long to see you but I know that may never happen – you are always close to me in spirit.

So, for news of Columba. Soldiers are gossips and since Constantine and Licinius sent letters across the empire telling everyone that the persecutions must end, we have become much friendlier with them. They have a grapevine and they told me that Columba has gained a reputation across many miles. He did eventually get to Rome and of course changed sides when Maxentius defeated Severus, who he started out under – the last I heard he ended up in Constantine's army as a legate in charge of 5,000 men. He nearly deserted but changed his mind when he got hold of some of the booty from Constantine's campaigns – broaches, clasps and rings. Columba is known most of all for his ambition and blood lust. Just a year before the persecution ended, they say he slaughtered the largest number of Franks in the theatre in Trier when the legion celebrated Constantine's victory in Gaul. But more than this, Viviana, he has now declared himself to be a follower of the Christian God, the God who wins the emperor's battles for him! He is not a true follower, for murder, theft and bloodshed are not the marks of someone who trusts in our Lord. If the emperor changes his god, so will Columba.

Now the persecutions are over, at least for the moment, please will you write to me with your news? Your words are like jewels – they free my soul. I long to hear more about your life. Oh, that we might meet once more!

With all my love and greetings in the Lord.

Clara

John arrived at the elders' meeting. They were an eclectic group, which they were very proud of because they wanted the church to welcome people from all walks of life. Only men could qualify to be an elder or a deacon.

Silas was the son of a wealthy Greek trader from Corinth. His background was not fully transparent as he had only moved to Antioch two years previously to enhance his business opportunities; he was in the oil and spice trade, distributing them from the East to Alexandria and Rome. He had risen quickly in the church, and spoke with an imposing voice. His wife had formerly been one of his own slaves. He had granted her freedom in order to legitimise their marriage as she had no money to offer as a payment to obtain the required 'free' status. The other slaves in his household continued on as slaves now under her authority.

John's own family had had a close link with the church at Antioch from the earliest times and he was particularly aware that it was here that the followers of Christ had been referred to as *Christians*. His family had gradually shed itself of its Jewish traditions over the last 200 years, partly because of the restrictions placed on the Jews by the ruling Romans. John himself had amassed his money through constructing swimming pools for the wealthier classes in Antioch.

The elders had been asked by a member of the church what the gospel had to say about slavery. This would be the main item for prayer and discussion. Stephen was single and had spent several years hiding in the desert, studying the teaching of Marcion, who characterised the Old Testament God as vengeful rather than compassionate. He had also made a detailed study of St Paul's letters to Timothy. He began by summarising a section from Paul's letter to Timothy concerning slavery. He said slaves should accept the authority of their masters in order to preserve the reputation of the faith, whether the masters were believers or not.[28]

Stephen started to speak. 'My brothers, it is clear that God himself is honoured through the proper respect given to a slave's master by his slave – they should be obedient and work in humble servitude. Masters have authority over their slaves and should exercise that authority as unto the Lord. As St Paul says, being an overseer is "a noble task".'[29]

All the elders bowed their heads, and then Silas spoke. 'As you already know, my wife was my former slave. She has crossed over from being under my authority as a slave to being under my authority as my wife. And she in turn has authority over the slaves in our household. So it is within the Church – as our Lord's flock, we are appointed to

28.   1 Timothy 6:1-2.
29.   1 Timothy 3:1.

exercise authority over church members to ensure that they do not stray into false teachings or immoral behaviour: so God exercises his authority through us. And so, John, I think it behoves us as the church elders to ask you why your son, Benedict, one of our deacons, has not instructed his wife to remain in church when those who have to do penance leave the service before the Eucharist is taken?'

John gathered his thoughts with a frown before raising his head. He had carefully prepared his speech. 'Benedict does not see that his duty to the church is greater than his feelings for his wife and her guardians. This is a matter of great sorrow for me. It has given me a great deal of anguish and I have prayed constantly to the Lord for an answer. He seems to think there is a difference between neutrality in the face of pagan worship and passing the names of other believers to the authorities, which he tells me Simon and Lydia did *not* do. Benedict is not suited to the discipline which is needed for the position of deacon. I want to sincerely extend my sorrow to you, my fellow elders, that such a circumstance has arisen and for any part I have played in promoting the possibility of him becoming a deacon in the first instance. I could of course tell him to instruct Viviana not to go to the church door with Simon and Lydia, but if he does so begrudgingly, will that resentment come out in a different way? And if it were so, to do that would create more unrest inside the church. I do not want to see the fellowship of believers damaged more than it has been.

'I have a possible solution which I want to bring before you. Benedict is very shy, but he is also very clever with words and able to argue with heretics and philosophers, beating back their pretentions that our Lord and Saviour was only partially divine, if at all.

'I believe I could encourage him to resign from his position as deacon and seek your recommendation to send him and his family to the church in Alexandria where many thinkers are trying to undermine the idea that God the Father, God the Son and God the Holy Spirit are of one substance. As you know, the apostle John has written this: "In the beginning was the Word, and the Word was with God, and the Word was God. He was with God in the beginning.'"[30]

The meeting was brought to a close with an agreement to pray over the issue and meet again the following week. The elders eventually decided that the least damage would be done through accepting John's proposal and within six weeks Benedict and Viviana, who was five months into her pregnancy, sailed for Alexandria. Their belongings were few but the most important item was a letter of recommendation to one of the churches there from the elders. The letter did not mention any difficulties but simply said that the elders believed Benedict had a crucial role to play in protecting the Church from heresy.

---

30. John 1:1-2.

PART 3

The Nicene Creed

Chapter Nine

A Surprise Visit: Early in the Year 325 in Nicomedia

Columba looked immaculate, with his shoulder armour tightly shaped over his muscular frame; his white tunic, red-crested helmet and bronze shin protectors all conveyed an authority in a sphere which was far removed from the everyday lives of most people. Still wearing his general's uniform, even though he had been promoted to one of Emperor Constantine's closest associates, Columba had just completed a special assignment. It followed the emperor's final crushing of Licinius in the regions surrounding the narrow channel between the Black Sea and the Mediterranean. The uneasy relationship between Constantine and Licinius had finally been broken beyond repair when Constantine's incursions against barbarian tribes were seen by Licinius as a threat against his dominions. Once again Constantine's strategic superiority on the battlefield prevailed and Licinius was defeated.

The bloodstained uniform which Columba had recently worn had been thrown away. The image in his mind which would not leave him was the emperor's face when he had related how, with a few men, he had gained entry into Licinius' almost empty palace and stabbed his wife and children to death while they slept. The emperor's face was, in fact, unmoved, despite Columba hoping he would hear the news with a smile of satisfaction. Columba knew that his life could be easily dispensed with if he were to boast publicly about his exploits.

The emperor, like Columba, saw murder as an almost everyday political necessity. His concern was overwhelmingly about the stealth needed to preserve his apostolic image. He was *God's representative* on earth and as such had to remain distant from the gory hands which pulled out the swords from the dying family members of his latest opponent. Emperor Constantine thought nothing of taking life, but he did not want the screams of the dying to be heard by anyone except the victims and the killers themselves; that was Columba's task and Columba would live or die depending on how successful he was.

Clara stared at Columba in disbelief – here he was in her doorway. *Why has he come here? Is Viviana dead? What does he want?*

She was terrified but did not want to show Columba her fear. 'What brings you back here?' she said quietly, trying to stop herself shaking. It was nearly twenty years since she had last seen him – his torso was god-like and he started to speak in a tone which was both distant and familiar at the same time. He walked in, and sat on the only chair in the room without invitation, taking his helmet off.

'Do not be afraid,'[31] he said, mimicking the words of Christ in John's Gospel. 'I am not here to harm you – you have nothing that I want or need.'

Clara immediately knew he was lying. He continued.

'The emperor is moving to the new city of Constantinople near here. I am one of his councillors, and if you have not already heard, I have risen to great heights in the army, first as legate and then a general – but it was my fearlessness that caught the emperor's eye. Didn't I say I would return? Have you forgotten?'

Clara thought to herself: *No, I have not forgotten*

Columba continued, unaware of his own arrogance. In any event, it was a badge that he was proud to wear. 'What has happened to Viviana? Did she return here after leaving me on the boat at Seleucia?'

---

31. John 14:27.

Clara instantly felt protective towards Viviana, but she did not know how much Columba already knew. Was he just toying with her? 'No, she never came back, Columba. Why did you separate?'

Columba thought for a moment. 'She could not continue to act as my wife as we had agreed. I think she wanted to be rid of me.'

Clara was surprised by his frankness and was about to tell Columba what Viviana had said in her letter when she thought better of it. Columba made no move to leave.

'What do you mean, Columba? She is your sister – you were just pretending, weren't you?'

Clara momentarily felt she had the upper hand but it was short lived: 'Viviana did not want to pretend to be my wife even for her own sake – had she told the truth we would have been thrown overboard or put aside at the nearest stopping place. Pretending is more than lying next to someone – you said *pretend*, not play act. She is completely self-deceived; gods would not be gods if they thought the most important thing in life was not thinking too much of themselves. That would be like an army gathering up men and weapons for a long campaign and then surrendering before the battle is even fought. She is a disgrace to our family...'

Columba stopped himself before saying too much, but he had said enough for Clara to know he was not simply visiting his aunt. She knew he could see her suspicions had been heightened; he believed she could not sense his continual inner twisting and turning. He saw every conversation as a struggle for supremacy.

In that strange space between feeling vulnerable and determination not to give way, Clara broke the silence.

'Why have you come here, Columba? I do not understand what you are looking for, or what I have to give to you. You seek power –

I have none. You gain nothing from simple everyday togetherness and why do you say *our family* when you despise us?'

Columba thought for a moment before replying.

'I have no family except you and Viviana. I do not know how many children I have, or how many women I have had. If having a soul means caring for them, then I do not have one – for me to care is weakness, and so I cannot see God as humble. Have you not heard how the emperor dreamt of a vision of Christ the night before the battle of Milvian Bridge, how our God told him to fight under the name of Christ, and how he saw those letters in the sky?'

Clara jumped in. '*Our God*? What are you saying?'

Columba was quick to reply. 'You already know that I covered myself in blood and glory when the emperor defeated the Franks, don't you, Clara? You have talked to the soldiers here, and I have also – let me tell you, Clara, that there is no such feeling as murder and destruction; it gives you a power and a sense of mastery that caring never can. You become a god in the act of execution. The blood of your victims becomes the water of life.

'So Christians say that weakness is at the heart of a powerful God's character and they use the cross and the resurrection to explain it. But the real glory is to come when judgement comes – when fire and eternal hell will resound throughout the world. Who will be saved? Not the people who care, but the people who win.'

Now Columba was in full flow; the years had made him into an articulate speaker. He was used to listening to orations from generals, noblemen and even the emperor himself.

'God is not scared of judgement, and neither am I! That is my god. Yes, your God and my god have the same name but they are two different gods! They are like twins but one is like Romulus and one is like Remus. Remus wanted Rome to be built in a different place but Romulus got his way – he murdered his own twin. My god is Romulus, yours is Remus...'

Columba had stirred up enough energy in himself to reveal the true purpose of his visit. Clara could see that he believed that everyone was corruptible and that Clara was no exception.

'You watch out, Clara, for if you are still alive, you will be royalty. Viviana is lost to such glory, wherever she is. I do not care. But you, Clara, when the time is right and the emperor is waning, could be a great ally for me; you will be my ears and eyes. Clara, move with me into the palace and take over the cleaning of the emperor's clothing and fabric. There is no one better than you, so the local nobles say, and you will assist me through the mist of intrigue which is always in the air. I want you to get close to Faustas and Crispus, the emperor's wife and stepson. They do not sing songs and play games when the emperor is away on his campaigns – they plot and plan . . . I do not trust any of the emperor's other advisors – I need you there, Clara.'

Clara now knew why he had come; not out of affection or memory, but simply to use her. She asked herself whether she wanted to live in a palace when she would be always wondering what kind of predator was creeping up behind her. Fear left her and she felt grateful that at last she could tell Columba who she was.

'Columba, my life is an ordinary one – often I feel hard done by and worn down by the drudgery I endure so I can pay for my daily bread. But to exchange it for a life of secrecy and whispered lies, even if my bed is surrounded by pillars and curtains, is for me like stepping off a high ledge into quicksand. I will not see the finery around me; I will not think how privileged I am because I will be overwhelmed with fear, yes, fear! I will be constantly looking over my shoulder. I cannot live like that.

'I do not find satisfaction like you in the thought of having power over others; it is not something I yearn for. For you, power over others is everything, whether the people you conquer are good or bad – for you, good people deserve to be trampled on, just like your mother was. I cannot be that person, Columba, much as you want me to be. Yes, your power destroys lives – I call that evil, you call it good – God is the judge, not me ...

'Columba, people will always find a way to care for one another just as they will to harm and kill – but whatever you think, Christ did not come to mastermind butchery on the battlefield. Whatever the emperor did or did not see in his dream doesn't matter – we all know history will be rewritten to brighten his image, anyway.' Clara stopped; she knew she had reached the point of no return.

Columba slowly put his helmet back on and rose from the chair. Clara had confirmed everything he had suspected: 'If you are content to drown in a tub of urine-soaked laundry then I will leave you to it. If I hear any reports of this conversation from anyone, then get the bath ready – you will not see the face of the man who holds your head down. If that is God's mercy, then you are welcome to it.'

He walked past Clara deliberately dropping a gold coin on the floor as he went out. On the coin were two identical faces, one of Emperor Constantine and one of Sol Invictus, the Protector of the Empire and the God of the Sun. The heads were both the same size and together facing in the same direction.

'One day that will be my head,' he said.

Chapter Ten
Setting Out

My dear Clara

I have not heard from you for a long time. Please let me know when you have received this – perhaps you can send a message through the church as we used to do, rather than relying on soldiers moving from one part of the empire to another. The believers in Nicomedia, Antioch and Alexandria often visit one another. I really hope my letters to you have not ended up in the wrong hands.

But first let me say again what happened from the time I left you.

In Antioch I was made to marry in accordance with the apostle Paul's instructions to Timothy. The apostle wrote that younger widows – they counted me as one even though I was not a widow – should marry so as not to be a burden to the church and fall prey to sensual desires.

Benedict is the son of an elder, John, in the church at Antioch. Benedict is a very mild, gentle character; when we were first married, he was painfully shy but he has courage deep down. He understood why I wanted to support Simon and Lydia when they were made to do penance at the church door for trading with the Romans during the persecution. He stood up to his father but there were great difficulties – so we moved to Alexandria. If we had not done that, Benedict would have had to resign as a deacon and his father, an elder in the church, would have lost credibility. So his father sent him here to Alexandria to help in the theological debates. Many eminent scholars come to Alexandria where there is a famous library. Benedict is a scribe and researcher for the Bishop of Alexandria whose name is Alexander.

At the moment Benedict is studying the work of Origen (a man so devout that he castrated himself in order to offer himself more fully to God). I know that the emperor has had enough of the arguments inside the Church and is calling a conference at Nicaea. They have tried a few Councils of Bishops to sort it out but now our bishop has excommunicated a man called Arius because he won't sign up to the bishop's own view. Almost 100 of his followers have also been excluded and they cannot attend any church anywhere in all the surrounding provinces. The emperor thinks that if these arguments carry on he might start losing battles.

Clara, we are travelling to Nicaea as Benedict is one of the best scribes they have. I will see you – yes, I will see you – my heart is leaping for joy. I pray that I will find you well. I cannot wait until the time comes. You will meet your namesake, Clara – her second name is Phyllis – she will be eleven later this year and her brother, Simon, is six. How they are looking forward to meeting you. I now clean the laundry for Bishop Alexander and his secretary, Athanasius, so I will be busy but every moment with you will be like manna from heaven . . .

Viviana finished her letter and showed it to Benedict later, after he returned when the children were asleep. He nodded in appreciation and sat against the wall with his head tilted to the side; he was weary. Viviana's joy at the prospect of seeing Clara again had brought a light and vigour to her face that Benedict had not seen for a while. Benedict began to say why he was feeling burdened. They were not travelling all the way to Nicaea just to see a theological argument debated. If Arius and the Bishop of Caesarea and their supporters won over the emperor, they would not be able to return to their home. Alexander and Athanasius would be exiled and there may even be violence.

He drew breath. 'I am sorry to burden you with all my woes, Viviana. You know so much more than I do about what goes on in the human heart. Nicaea will be a turning point, but we can only wait on the Lord. He has been merciful to us thus far.'

Viviana sat still for a while and then, with a half-smile, said, 'Benedict, you might even have to become a laundry worker like me – fetching, carrying and treading. Come, Benedict, let us rest.'

As they lay down, they both sensed that each other were awake. Viviana slowly rested her head on Benedict's shoulder and quietly their minds stilled; eventually they fell asleep. When they began to pack their possessions for the journey, the knowledge that they might not return played on their minds. Viviana decided to take the small wooden cross her mother had given her rather than keep it at home for safety.

As the cargo ship caught the gentle breeze leaving the bustling cosmopolitan port, the children looked in wonder at the immense lighthouse tower standing defiantly in the sea. Alexandria faded into the distance.

'Has it been there forever?' Simon asked his father.

'No, Simon, it was built 600 years ago,' Benedict replied.

The sound of the sea gradually increased; the fading noise of the city and the many shades of terracotta merged into a single grey mass. As the light winds took the grain-filled ship away from the port, the groans and sighs of the slave rowers vividly reminded Viviana of the original journey she had taken with Columba from Nicomedia. Her heart ached.

Viviana and Benedict had decided not to travel with the other bishops and Church officials on the army horses provided by the emperor to Nicaea; it was unusual for children to travel by sea but Benedict had enough money to pay the captain for the journey. Travel by sea would be quicker than by land, but more than that, they wanted to visit Antioch on the way. While in Alexandria, Benedict had felt a sense of duty towards his father; they had exchanged letters but only very brief ones, establishing that they were both still well. Benedict's father was very reluctant to say anything about the church in Antioch, choosing rather to quote parts of recent sermons that he had given. Benedict had wanted the children, Clara and Simon, to see him at least once, although he wondered what his father's disposition towards them would be.

Viviana, on the other hand, wanted to introduce the children to Simon and Lydia. Again, letters had been exchanged and remarkably, despite their years, they were still helping to make tents along with their sons who lived nearby. A year after Viviana and Benedict had left for Alexandria, Simon and Lydia had been allowed back into full communion at the church. Simon had approached John a few times to greet him but the replies had been clipped; he was polite but distant.

Although the coastal winds were generally against the direction of travel, most of the slave rowers were fit enough to row, and after nine days the port of Antioch came into sight. The family made their way to the house Benedict had grown up in and a servant answered the door. They were shown in and John stood there waiting.

'This is your grandfather, Clara and Simon,' Benedict said, intimating how they should respond.

'Papus,' they chorused as they had been prepared to say, and then they bowed.

John asked them, 'How many psalms can you repeat by heart?'

'Ten,' said Simon before Clara could signal to him to keep quiet.

Simon started to repeat one of them but faltered on the second line, getting the words muddled up. John immediately railed and looked at Benedict.

'You are ruining the boy. He should be beaten until he knows it off by heart. "Whoever spares the rod hates their children, but the one who loves their children is careful to discipline them."'[32]

John left the room instantly. For the rest of the day, John stayed in his room and when Benedict went to ask if he would eat with them, he said he was preparing to give a sermon on Sunday. After a stony breakfast Viviana and Benedict decided that it would be best if she and the children stayed with Simon and Lydia for a few days: difficult though it was, Benedict wanted to spend some time with his father.

Wondering what to do, he thought his father would relax a little if he asked him what he would be preaching about. Benedict knew that John found it very difficult to talk about family matters and was much more comfortable talking about the Old Testament scriptures and the letters from the apostles which circulated between the churches. Benedict remembered clearly how his father had changed years back after his mother had left the family home – he could not bear to reveal that he was deeply hurt, preferring to transfer his anger onto those believers whom he saw as heretical and disloyal.

John read out two texts to Benedict; the first was an Old Testament text which prohibited beating slaves to the point of death and confirmed that they were the owner's property.[33] The second was a

32.   Proverbs 13:24.
33.   Exodus 21:21.

letter from the apostle Peter, 'It is commendable if someone bears up under the pain of unjust suffering because they are conscious of God.'[34] He went on, 'My sermon will be based on the fact that our Lord took punishment even though it was unjustified, and if we are to witness effectively we should do the same. For that reason, God approves of slavery because it provides a model of how we should conduct ourselves. God, himself, used slavery to show his power in rescuing the children of Israel from the Egyptians.'[35]

Benedict knew from years of being made to listen to his father that he dare not say anything or question his father's judgement. 'Father,' he began tentatively. 'The passage from Exodus is part of the Scripture but the letter from Peter the apostle is not Scripture even though some say it should be. There are so many different lists of what could be included as divinely inspired that no one is certain. But there is a much bigger question to answer – did our Lord and Saviour come to enforce the law or change the way it is used?'

Benedict thought he had probably said enough, so he was more than taken aback when his father said, 'Go on. I'm listening.'

Benedict drew breath: 'And, Father, you remember Leviticus 19:18, of course: "Do not seek revenge or bear a grudge against anyone *among your people*, but love your neighbour as yourself. I am the LORD."[36] Well, the parable of the Good Samaritan[37] changed who our neighbours are – everyone – slaves included...'

Benedict did not think he could say anymore. His father simply arose and said, 'Goodnight, Benedict – may the Lord bless you and keep you.'

---

34. 1 Peter 2:19.
35. Exodus 6:1-8.
36. Emphasis author's.
37. Luke 10:25-37.

The next morning Benedict was expecting his father to at best remain silent and worse say something about regretting not having beaten him more when he was a child. The servant brought in the bread, cheese and olives. To drink, she fetched mulsum, a mixture of honey and wine with spices. Benedict paused before speaking again.

'Father, I don't want the children to remember you as an angry person – do you want to see them before we travel on to Nicaea?'

John thought for a moment. Benedict knew that his father could not express his feelings – but what he didn't know was that John could also not work out why he had felt a sudden burst of affection for his son. He lived in a world where thinking for oneself was a sin, a symptom of falling away from faith, but somehow Benedict had broken through it without diminishing his faith.

John looked up with a gentler look in his eyes.

'Bring them here to eat tomorrow, and also Simon and Lydia.'

Chapter Eleven
Nicaea

As the ship creaked out of the Antioch harbour, Viviana stood on the deck reflecting on what had been, in the end, a life-affirming visit. The meal at John's started very awkwardly but gradually his strident voice had faded away, his stern expression changing into mellow watchfulness. Simon and Lydia had wondered why they had been invited. They thought John might take the opportunity to reprimand them again, but despite that they had told Viviana they wanted to be there for her. The children had been primed to say nothing and only speak when questioned. Little Simon had learned a psalm off by heart and Clara hardly looked up. By the end of the evening the children were playing a game with their hands, putting one on top of the other as quickly as possible. They were laughing and John watched on with the faintest of smiles. That was something Benedict had never imagined possible.

Viviana knew that the visit would have a deep resonance for Benedict, not just because of his difficult relationship with his father but also because of the unspoken absence of his mother. More than twenty years earlier she had gone to live with one of the nobles John had been building for. John never spoke about the matter to Benedict, who knew not to raise the subject. Benedict and Viviana had told the children she had left many years ago and now lived a long way away. In fact, she lived just outside Antioch at a wealthy equestrian's house, having nothing to do with the church. Even those locals who knew of her would never speak to John about her, and he could never bring himself to enquire. Viviana did not know if Benedict had tried to see her while they had been in Antioch.

When she later asked him, he told her he had found himself walking towards where he thought she lived, but then turned back for the sake of his father. He had wanted to see his mother if only to reassure himself that she was alright, but he could not do that at the expense of causing his father distress. Since his mother left, it seemed it had never crossed John's mind that Benedict might want to see her. Benedict could have resented his father but he did not; he felt sorry for him. He was, after all, the only parent he now knew; in any event, children would normally live with the father, providing he had servants, if the mother left home for another. Benedict thought that whatever anger, shame and humiliation his father had hidden inside himself must have contributed to his belief that sin could be beaten out of people. Perhaps that recent conversation, the only real one he had ever had with his father, would open the door to others in the future – Benedict knew he wanted to see him again.

One evening, Benedict began to muse with Viviana about Christ's reverence for his Father in heaven; he compared it with his relationship with John. He also thought about his son, Simon, running around in a very small space on the deck. For a moment he tried to imagine how he would have felt if he had been Abraham being asked by God to sacrifice his son Isaac as an offering.[38] Benedict was familiar with the prohibition against child sacrifice in Deuteronomy,[39] so it had never made sense to him why God asked Abraham to do such a thing in the first place, even allowing for the last-minute change of mind. It was a perplexing mystery, but Benedict knew in his heart that he would never intentionally harm his own son. He was thinking about all of this not just because of their recent visit to Antioch, but because it was connected to the major issue at the forthcoming Bishop's

---

38. Genesis 22:1-19.
39. Deuteronomy 18:9-12.

Council. He asked Viviana a question: 'The bond between Christ and his heavenly Father cannot be like the one between us and Clara and Simon, can it?'

It was the kind of question Viviana was used to thinking about. Women were not thought to be capable of teaching in churches, but Benedict knew otherwise.

'Clara and Simon are innocent, not because everything they say and do is kind, but because they are changing – they are growing up – they have not reached a place where their understanding of the world is more or less set. Christ had his earthly parents – they worried about him when he stayed at the temple without them knowing.[40] I do not know, nor does anyone really know, how Christ was God, but I often ask myself, "How could God truly understand a broken, hateful and suffering world without experiencing it himself?"'

Benedict loved Viviana and was constantly amazed by her wise words.

'You are right, Viviana! I also think that Christ was in some way God himself even though Christ often spoke about his Father and prayed to him.'

Viviana was silent. The sound of the waves and the strange moonlight filtering through the floating clouds somehow offered them a sense of solace; the world around was an incomparable force which could not be understood with words alone; it was unfathomable, just like the invisible force that bound them to each other and the children. Viviana pondered about that togetherness – it was both vulnerable and profound.

The days were long and every evening they all huddled together in a sheltered corner of the deck, listening to the sound of the sea and the heavy sighs of the rowers. Their sleep was fitful as they headed closer

---

40. Luke 2:41-52.

to Nicomedia, but the wind was generally in a favourable direction and that brought the prospect of seeing the harbour ever closer.

It was twenty years since Viviana had seen the harbour at Nicomedia fade away behind her. As the ship now approached the landing, the excitement of the children took her attention away from everything that had happened to her since. Among the many carts, mules and slaves were those masters and officials whose voices and brighter coloured tunics marked them out from the crowd. Viviana took a second look at a figure as the ship veered back and forth trying to come in sideways as near as possible before ropes were thrown from the deck. She seemed familiar even after all these years and it was unmistakably Clara. Her angular face was slightly thinner but her complexion was still tanned; she had always been slight and wiry with dark-brown hair. She was smiling and crying at the same time, and wore a scarf over her head and shoulders with a long pale tunic dress. As Viviana stepped onto dry land they embraced for what seemed an age and the children joined in the hug.

Benedict stood by until eventually Viviana introduced him. It was a joyful meeting and the children were exuberant with their newfound great-aunt – they instantly felt accepted by her smile; it was as if she was a grandmother. Although Clara had her reasons for wanting to remain unnoticed, the children ran around jumping for joy. The local grapevine would absorb the news of the family's arrival very quickly.

The troubles of life faded away as they walked back, laughing and crying. The children wanted to know about the noble families Clara laundered for, their houses, horses and statues. They squeezed into Clara's two rooms and after they had eaten, the children eventually settled down to sleep in the other room.

Benedict seemed to feel he should leave Viviana and Clara to talk, knowing the history and how close they were. He looked awkward, both a bystander and a participant. Clara sensed his diffidence and asked him about their plans to help him relax a little.

'Our time is much shorter than we would like, Clara,' Benedict replied. 'We have to stay in Nicaea, thirty miles away, so Viviana can do the laundry for Bishop Alexander and his understudy, Athanasius.'

'Ah!' said Clara, laughing. 'So I have taught you something useful after all, Viviana.'

Benedict smiled at the joke and went on to explain that he was there to keep notes for Bishop Alexander and Athanasius at the council. He casually said that the emperor would attend the beginning of the council. Clara's face visibly changed.

'What is it?' Viviana asked.

Clara replied in a quiet way. She did not want Viviana to sense any of the fear which she had lived with since Columba's visit, but it was to no avail.

'I had a visit from Columba. He is now one of the emperor's special guards and lives at the palace. He asked me to go to the palace to help with the emperor's laundry . . . but really he wanted me to feed him with information. He still has ambitions to climb higher. He lives in a world of conspiracy, lies and violent intent. If the emperor comes, Columba might be there too. I told him that I would never do what he wanted, and he left with a sneer, telling me not to breathe a word to anyone – but he is not someone who forgets a rebuff, is he? And the children . . . ?'

That night Viviana could not sleep, her mind spinning with the same thoughts coming back again and again. She imagined that he was standing over her and she was looking up at him saying, *You can only kill . . . you deal in fear but what if, Columba, your spell doesn't touch me? Your only weapon is blunted ... your body is strong but your heart is dead! I am not scared of you even if you kill me, because you will be alone, and that is your punishment. You will always be alone.'* But once she had rehearsed that speech two or three times, she realised that confronting him would only increase the risk of him seeking revenge and for that, the children would be his target.

Viviana came to her senses. *I will have to find a way. He thinks I am weak, that I cannot match his guile, but to protect my children I will have to find his Achilles heel.*

She woke Clara – it was about five o'clock in the morning, an hour or so before Clara would set off to collect the laundry from the nobleman's house. Clara yawned but realised Viviana wanted to talk.

'You are right to be fearful, Clara. Columba only understands the language of threat.'

Clara did not need reminding, for she had hardly slept herself. They exchanged ideas.

'Is it wrong to play him at his own game? Should we protect ourselves or leave it to the Lord?' asked Clara.

'We have to do something without being dragged into Columba's world.'

'What is his weakness, Viviana? Not cruelty – not guilt – but his quest for more and more power ... How can we make sure he leaves us all – especially the children – alone?'

Simon came running in.

'I heard you talking, Mummy! What are you talking about?'

'Nothing you need worry about, Simon. Come here and we can rest together,' Viviana said.

Simon came and rested alongside his mother and briefly he fell back to sleep.

Two days later the family left for Nicaea, the emperor's soldiers had been ordered to assist in the travel arrangements for the bishops and those with them. Benedict and Viviana were provided with two horses; young Clara mounted up with Viviana and Simon was lifted onto the saddle with Benedict. Two soldiers accompanied them with their belongings for the thirty-mile journey.

Once they had left, Clara sent a message through one of the local soldiers to Columba; the message was that Clara would like to see him. Five days later Columba arrived at her door.

'So, Clara,' he smirked. 'You have seen sense.'

Clara looked at him without a shred of foreboding. 'This letter is for you – please read it.'

Columba took the letter and opened it.

To Columba

The gospel is about finding strength through weakness – it is not about exploiting weakness. All you see is blood.

This is to tell you that if any member of my family, my husband, me and the children, my husband's family and our aunt Clara, or any of those close to us experience injury, death or disaster which you are suspected of being behind, the emperor will be given details of your ambitions and attempts to create an informer network.

The person who will pass this information to the emperor in the event of the above happening is known only to me, Viviana, your sister, and if I am harmed, the message will be immediately sent. If you make any attempt to trace them, the emperor will be sent a message.

Your sister

Viviana

Columba looked up in disbelief. He laughed: 'Do you think such an empty threat bothers me?'

Clara replied, 'Yes, I do. Just leave, Columba.'

As Clara looked out down below on the street, Columba was burning the letter.

Chapter Twelve
The Creed

We believe in One God, the Father Almighty, Maker of all things visible and invisible:

And in one Lord Jesus Christ, the Son of God, begotten of the Father, Only-Begotten, that is, *from the essence of the Father* : God from God, Light from Light, Very God from Very God, begotten not made, *one in essence with the Father*, by Whom all things were made, both things in heaven and things on earth; Who for us men and for our salvation came down and was made flesh, was made man, suffered, and rose again the third day, ascended into heaven, and cometh to judge the quick and the dead.

And in the Holy Ghost

And those who say 'Once he was not' and 'Before His generation He was not' and 'He came to be from nothing' or those who pretend that the Son of God is 'of other substance or essence', or 'created' or 'alterable' or 'mutable', the Catholic Church (meaning the universal church) anathematizes.[41]

The Nicene Creed stated that Christ and the Father were of exactly the same essence; as if a lump of bread dough had been divided up into three different shapes, Father, Son and Holy Spirit. The followers of Arius saw it more like the fermentation of wine, with the wine being

---

41. Bishop of Caesaria's letter to his diocese immediately following the Council of Nicaea, as recorded by Church historians Socrates and Theodoret. See Patrick Whitworth, *Defining God: Athanasius, Nicaea and the Trinitarian Controversy of the Fourth Century* (Durham: Sacristy Press, 2023), p. 67. Please note that the authenticity of the last paragraph is disputed by some scholars. To 'anathematize' is to condemn.

fermented a second time to make vinegar; the Father came first and the Son followed on. The priest Arius and his followers, those who believed Christ was a heavenly messenger sent by God to save the world, would soon be forced to leave Alexandria and its surrounds.

For a moment the Church looked united; close to 300 bishops had come from throughout the empire and only two refused to sign with their agreement. The grand opening of the council had seen the emperor enter with a divine resplendence that no one could miss. The Bishop of Caesarea would later write in glowing tones how the emperor resembled a messenger from heaven. The Bishop of Nicomedia would introduce the emperor to the assembly in deferential tones, making every effort to engender an atmosphere in which only submission was appropriate. Everyone knew that already.

Shortly after the council ended, Emperor Constantine invited the bishops to a celebration of his twenty-year rule, named *vicennalia*, in Nicomedia where Clara lived. And so Benedict, Viviana and the children were able to see Clara again for a short while before returning to Alexandria with Bishop Alexander and his secretary, Athanasius, at the emperor's expense. When the children were asleep, the three of them began to talk openly. Viviana had been hoping that Clara might come to live with them in Alexandria. Clara had thought through the prospect beforehand.

'Nothing would please me more, but I cannot be under the same roof as all of you in case Columba comes to harm us. If his quest for greater power fails, he may just take revenge on us anyway. If he kills anyone it will probably be me first, and a message will have to be passed to you, Viviana.'

'You do not have to do that! The letter to Columba will not stop him from coming for us wherever we are,' Viviana replied. 'You can come with us, can't she, Benedict?'

Benedict was instant in his response: 'Of course – absolutely – without you, Clara, Viviana would have either perished or become a slave. Come with us, Clara . . . do.'

Clara responded again: 'I would if it were not for the children. If Columba comes for me, I will not tell him anything. One of my helpers will find me and tell someone in the church here; they will send a message to you in Alexandria as quickly as possible and then you can decide what to do.'

Viviana thought herself into that scenario, imagining that she had received a letter telling her that Clara had been killed at the hands of Columba. What would be uppermost in her mind: her anger against Columba for murdering Clara? Or would it be the fear that Columba would kill the children to inflict pain on her – or simply the fear of his unrelenting hatred? They were unimaginable thoughts.

She embraced Clara, and slowly all three of them bowed their heads and prayed silently.

Two days later Benedict, Viviana and the children left. The emperor's horses came and tearful farewell words and embraces were exchanged. As Viviana looked back after a few hundred yards she saw a group of soldiers standing near the building where Clara lived. She looked back again; the figures were too far away for her to pick out but as she travelled on, she kept trying to picture them again. She kept on asking herself if one of them was Columba.

The family arrived back in Alexandria. The bishop, Alexander, was weakening and his secretary, Athanasius, was beginning to take over. In the meantime, Benedict simply carried out his duties.

One evening after a meal, Simon looked at Benedict.

'Yes, Simon?' Benedict said.

'How many Fathers did Jesus have?' he asked.

Chapter Thirteen

'All Who Draw the Sword Will Die by the Sword'[42]

Eighteen months later, Benedict penned an important letter to his father in Antioch.

Dear Father

Greetings in the Lord.

Since the Council of Nicaea, many of the bishops have convinced the emperor that they should be readmitted to the Church and there is a council to take place in Nicomedia in the not-too-distant future, which could well see Bishop Alexander and his secretary, Athanasius, exiled. The emperor is not mindful of which doctrine is taught by the Church – it is of no concern to him. It seems the Arians, who believe Christ only came into being on earth, now have the emperor's ear. If the bishop is exiled we too will have to leave, as we are his staff. Father, I am writing to ask if at least for the moment we could stay with you in Antioch. I would seek work and Viviana would be there to prevent the children from disturbing you.

We await your reply.

Your son

Benedict

John's letter arrived four weeks later, carried to Alexandria by a member of the church at Antioch.

---

42. Matthew 26:52. Capitals in the heading are mine.

Dear Benedict

Please do come and stay with me. I have only one servant now who has chosen to remain with me. I have sent the other back to her homeland. Viviana would have to help with some of the additional household duties. I will make enquiries regarding work for you.

I will expect you. Please send a message as to when you are coming.

In his grace

Your father

A soldier knocked on Clara's door, shouting out her name. She and her helpers were outside treading the laundry but were distracted by the shouting. Clara came round the front of the block and called the soldier down.

'I'm here – what do you want?' she said.

'My name is Beatus,' he said. 'I have some news for you.'

They both came inside after Clara left instructions with her helpers about what to do next with the laundry.

'Well?' said Clara.

Beatus was quite short and burly. He had blond hair and like Columba, wore a uniform of high rank. His chiselled face had a long scar running down one side of it and his teeth were uneven. He told Clara how he had originally met Columba, how they met again in Rome, changing allegiances until they became allied to Constantine.

After the recent Council of Nicaea and the *vicennalia* celebration, Columba had caught wind of some treachery involving Crispus, the emperor's son, and Fausta, the emperor's wife. He told the emperor something which made him very angry and Helena, Emperor

Constantine's mother, also became entwined. Even though Crispus had greatly helped his father defeat Licinius, many rumours about conspiracies abounded. For one thing, Constantine's wife, Fausta, seeing how well Crispus, her stepson, was doing, was concerned about her own sons being overshadowed. No one knew if the emperor suspected that something was going on between Crispus and Fausta.

Clara looked impassive but wondered if Beatus had been sent by Columba to deceive her into revealing what she knew about Viviana's threat. The awful thought of her being tortured crossed her mind. Where was it all leading?

Beatus continued, 'The emperor despatched both Columba and me to bring about the eternal disappearance of Crispus, his wife and child, Fausta and many other friends. Columba and I kill for a living and the emperor does not want his holy reputation stained with the details being known. I know Columba came to see you, and what you hear from me is also bound by the same threat – if you disclose anything your life will be in peril – not from Columba because he is dead, but from me.'

Clara gasped and waited for more. She wondered instantly if she was being told the truth and felt her body stiffen with anxiety.

'The emperor took audiences with both me and Columba after we returned from Pola[43] where Crispus perished,' Beatus went on. 'We had been away for several months. Columba told the emperor that I had dealt with Fausta by arranging for her to be put into a boiling hot bath. I knew that Columba had been with Fausta before arranging for her to take a bath in case she was pregnant – whether she died from the bath or by some other means, I am not sure.

'When my turn came to speak with the emperor, he asked me what I had done with Fausta. It was my life or Columba's, so I told the

---

43. Pola is a coastal town in modern day Croatia, about 1,000 miles from Nicomedia.

emperor what I knew, that it was Columba who had been with Fausta and brought about her end. The emperor listened and looked at me. He said, 'Only one of you is telling the truth.' I bowed and retired, walking backwards out of the chamber knowing that would not be the end of it. I could not risk Columba telling more lies about me so he could protect himself.

'Immediately after seeing the emperor, Columba and I went with two servant girls, only I pretended and kept my knife close by. When Columba was in the act, I stabbed him from behind and he perished. I remember his face as he turned round; he looked surprised. I said to him as he gasped the last few breaths of his life, "I did not kill Fausta – you did." I finished the task, wiped some of the blood away with his tunic – here it is – and then I called some guards to dispose of the body secretly.' He threw the tunic onto the floor.

'Why have you come to tell me all this?' Clara asked, stunned. 'Why haven't you kept it to yourself?'

'Columba told me when he returned from seeing you to ask you to live at the palace that you were the only person he knew who told the truth and kept their word,' Beatus replied, gently. 'I need someone to know the truth in case I am accused by one of Fausta's sons of bringing about her demise. They could turn on me, especially as I am the only one alive who carried out the emperor's punishments.' He reached out and touched her hand, briefly. 'That is why you have to know, but you are under an obligation to tell no one of this conversation unless you are asked about it by a representative of the emperor.' He lowered his voice. 'And I do not have to spell out what being under an obligation means, do I?'

With that, Beatus left. Clara stared at the floor and looked at the tunic, bloodstained and muddy. For several minutes she was still, not believing what she had just heard, and then it struck her that her two helpers were still outside with the laundry. She ran down to finish off the morning's work with them in a state of shock.

Over the next two weeks Clara sent two messages to the palace asking for Columba to visit her. He never came. She couldn't work out if Columba or Beatus had told the emperor the truth about the death of Fausta, but she knew now that Columba was dead.

Letters flowed between Clara and Viviana over the next few months. Benedict, Viviana and the children, Clara and Simon, had left Alexandria and moved into John's house. Viviana was more than happy to be close to Simon and Lydia, who had said that Clara in Nicomedia could come and live with them if she wanted to, now that the threat from Columba had gone. A few months later, Clara took up the offer. The deep lines on Clara's face showed the years of hard, unremitting labour but she felt a peace, a sense of relief, that after everything the family was somehow still intact. She was still strong enough to help with the lighter side of the tentmaking business that Simon and Lydia's sons had taken on, and often saw the children, Clara and Simon.

Clara's prayers had changed from desperation to hope:

I thank you God for Viviana, for my new life here in Antioch – for releasing me from Columba's grip – for the love Viviana has shown me.

Why are Viviana and Columba so different from one another? What was the affliction that beset Columba? Thank God his mother was not here to weep over him – I both despise him and feel pity for him – I cannot understand how those two feelings can live alongside one another. I know I cannot bring myself to forgive him as if he had done nothing – that is beyond me; what will become of little Simon? Please God, stop him from going down the same pathway.

John, Benedict's father, had given up preaching and stepped down from being an elder. He was secretly glad to have done so. He enjoyed reading stories from the Old Testament to Clara and Simon. One day John was reading from the book of Exodus.[44] He was telling them how the king of Egypt gave orders for all male babies of the Israelites to be put to death because the Jewish people were increasing in number.

Simon suddenly interjected, stopping John in his tracks. 'Clara told me that we had two brothers who died before I was born.'

'Shhhh,' said Clara. 'Papus does not know. I told you not to say anything.'

John looked up and paused for a moment, keeping his feelings of resignation to himself. Almost every family he knew had lost children. He continued with the story, explaining how the Jewish midwives did not kill the babies – they told the king that the babies had been born before the midwives arrived.

Undeterred, Simon said, 'When I grow up, I will become a soldier and kill those Egyptians. I will be very strong.'

John spoke quietly to him. 'Listen to your father, Simon – he knows our Lord wants us to care about other people as well as our own.'

Simon looked at his grandfather and later that day went to talk to Benedict about becoming a soldier.

John had found Benedict a post with the Bishop of Antioch, writing his letters and recording his sermons; Benedict was a brilliant secretary. However, Benedict had recently visited his mother without seeking permission from his father and had since spent many hours agonising over whether he should have done so.

---

44. See Exodus 1:15-22.

She looked different, like a nobleman's wife; as if she was always ready to please him at a moment's notice. She asked no questions about my life. I could not bring myself to say anything about the family; she had not wanted me to go there, and I won't go again. She was indifferent – cold – I felt the chill of an icy wind had struck my heart. Thank God in heaven for Viviana's understanding – so different from my mother. Should I tell my father about it in case he hears it from others? I am not sure.

Viviana had learned to embroider while she was doing the Bishop Alexander's laundry and now worked at home producing robes for the bishop and his staff. Viviana thought about her own mother when Benedict told her about his visit, and her whole life flashed before her:

I remember her face. I remember her holding me. I have heard about her end, not from Clara, but from others. I cannot understand why some people think they can take another person's life away from them; my two boys – they died from fevers, I saw them go – do you know what that is like, Lord? It was you who came to walk alongside us, and yet I don't know how you can understand a mother's grief at seeing her own child die? You had no children of your own, but I suppose everyone is your child. I cannot fathom it.

I thank you for Benedict, the children and Clara, Simon and Lydia and John too. Can you journey with us as you did on this earth? I have the gift of trusting you. I do not even know where it has come from. Despite my mother's cruel death and my two boys perishing, I still trust . . . I cannot believe that there is no one greater than me. I am too frail and fragile for that. I see you, Christ, talking to ordinary people. I cannot heal them or make food out of loaves and fishes, but I see you caring for them – listening, giving way – and then giving hope, somewhere we need to be loved. My mother loved me. I know you rose again, but I'm not sure I will. I cannot see that far. I am not sure what will happen to me. I am like the widow who gave a penny, not the man who wanted everyone else to see him praying...[45]

I do not see a plan – either behind or ahead. Columba's brutality took that away from me; I take one step at a time. Just as Mother would not have wanted Columba to have become a soldier, so I also do not want Simon to thirst after the excitement of killing... and where can we find another Benedict for our Clara? There are so many who bully their wives and then say it is your will.

Lord God, you said we must not murder,[46] so how can rulers boast about carrying out your will by killing others? If rulers do the very thing you command them not to, how can they put on the robes of your kingdom? My mother let her life be torn apart by rulers like that. Our emperor now worships you – does he? He kills too; has he had his reward already?[47] He can kill, conquer other lands, he can build palaces, he can have as many women as he chooses; he can do anything – he could even be baptised – but the one thing he cannot do is love, for there is no space in his heart for that. Just like Columba, who had all that power but in the end had nothing. Thank you, Lord, for your life... you have shown me that life is stronger than death, and that despite everything there is something called 'good' – thank you, Lord...

45.   Mark 12:41-44; Matthew 6:5-6.
46.   Exodus 20:13.
47.   Matthew 6:2.

Appendix One
Timeline

Timeline of the story – the main fictitious characters are in **bold**

289 – **Phyllis' husband, Bonitus,** *joins Diocletian to repel barbarians from the north.*

290 – **Phyllis' husband, Bonitus,** *returns injured and goes back to the front line.*

295 – **Phyllis** *becomes a Christian.*

302 – **Phyllis** *murdered in the amphitheatre (**Viviana** is fourteen, **Columba** is twelve, **Clara** is twenty-nine).*

305 – **Viviana and Columba** *leave for Alexandria but **Viviana** separates when they dock at Seleucia*

Brief Military History (306-313).

306 – *Maxentius in Rome claims the status of emperor and the eastern Augustus Severus is defeated by 307 – many of his troops change sides. Maxentius reverses the order to persecute Christians but Galerius and Maximian Daia continue on. The persecution is not universal but ends in 313.*

308 – *Licinius made emperor in the West by Diocletian and Galerius. Constantine nearly loses support of own troops as he vies with Maximian Daia (Maxentius' father). Booty from campaigns – brooches, clasps and rings – are distributed to soldiers by Constantine, which helps to keep them loyal. Coinage is minted which proclaim 'The Glory of the Gallic Army'.*

309 – *Constantine and Maximian Daia (who had joined Constantine in the west after losing out to his son Maxentius Daia in 308) battle in Marseille with no clear victor. Maximian dies by 310.*

311 – *Galerius dies. Maxentius claims patronage of Mars, Constantine claims patronage of Apollo.*

312 – *Battle of Milvian Bridge. Constantine defeats Maxentius, whose retreat over a collapsing bridge is fatal. Constantine is said to honour the Christian God for giving him the victory. Constantine goes back to Gaul and thousands of captive Franks are slaughtered in the arena at Trier.* **Columba** *catches the emperor's eye by reason of his ruthlessness.*

313 – *The Edict of Milan in 313, the end of persecution, is fashioned by Constantine and Licinius. It brings about a spate of new, ornate churches in Rome and the news spreads quickly across the Roman Empire. The empire is now shared between Constantine and Licinius.*

313 – **Viviana is twenty-five, Columba is twenty-three. Viviana marries Benedict. Clara is forty.**

314 – **Benedict and Viviana have a daughter, Clara.**

316-19 – **Viviana has two boys who die very young of fever.**

319 – **Benedict and Viviana have a son, Simon.**

324 – *Constantine murders Licinius and family and friends and becomes the sole emperor of the Roman Empire.*

325 – *Nicaea meeting of bishops when first Nicene Creed is produced.* **Viviana is thirty-seven and Columba, thirty-five.**

326 – *Constantine orders the murder of his wife, Fausta and stepson, Crispus.*

*327 – **Clara** joins family in Antioch where **Benedict's father, John, lives** after **Columba** is killed. The emperor reinstates those who believe Christ was temporal (i.e. not part of a timeless Godhead).*

It was not uncommon for people to live into their fifties or sixties or even more, but the average life span across the population was extremely low due to very high child and maternal mortality rates and basic or no medical intervention when people fell ill.

Appendix Two
Key Library Sources

Mary Beard, *SPQR: A History of Ancient Rome* (London: Profile Books, 2015).

Harry Y. Gamble, *The New Testament Canon: Its Making and Meaning* (Philadelphia, PA: Fortress Press, 1985)

Kenneth Scott Latourette, *A History of Christianity* (London: Eyre & Spottiswoode Limited, 1955)

Paul Stephenson, *Constantine: Unconquered Emperor, Christian Victor* (London: Quercus, 2011)

Patrick Whitworth, *Defining God: Athanasius, Nicaea and the Trinitarian Controversy of the Fourth Century* (Durham: Sacristy Press, 2023)

Also available

from www.malcolmdown.co.uk

The Daughter is set two thousand years ago around the time of Christ. A young girl, Rebekah, finds herself in a predicament – should she go along with the life her father and her Jewish community has set down for her? How much should she concern herself about the expectations of others? What will her mother feel if she takes a different road? If she runs away from the cruel man she is betrothed to will she just find herself destitute and die? Would it be better not to cause a fuss and make the best of it? At least she would have a roof over her head.

ISBN: 9781915046437

£10.99

In a time of turmoil and religious upheaval, a village in West Saxony stands witness to a brutal event that sends shockwaves through the lives of its inhabitants. Nathan Driscoll's *Reformation* takes us back to the heart of medieval Europe, where life hangs by a thread, with faith and fear fuelled by the ambitions of powerful men, morphing together.

ISBN: 9781915046871

£12.99